BRADY F**KING WITTER

A Movie Star Romance

CHRISTINE J DARCY

CONTENTS

PROLOGUE

HAVEN

I had a bad habit of roller skating down the Sunset Strip at midnight. I loved the neon signs, the orange glow of the tail lights as I sped by, the rock and roll music of Los Angeles playing against the beat of my heart.

It was dangerous on a regular day, but that day my world was collapsing in on me and I raced down the streets like I was running for my life. Pedestrians leapt out of the way, calling out expletives behind them as if I could hear anything beyond the sound of my heaving breath. If I could just get enough air, if I could just keep moving, then I wouldn't fall apart. But I was lying to myself. I knew if I stopped then that is exactly what I'd do. I'd collapse in a million hot jagged pieces that neither I nor anyone else would ever be able to put back together.

I wanted to blame him but, how could I? He gave me fair warning and I chose not to heed it. I could only blame myself. And, that made it so much worse.

I wanted to turn off my mind, the part of it that re-tread every word of our last conversation and all the conversations that preceded it. In the forefront of my mind, a mirage of him lingered, like a ghost I could never get behind me. The first time we looked at each other, when he kissed me, when he left me. I couldn't go fast enough. My long-tired skates beneath me rattled, likewise threatening to break apart.

"Wait," a voice said. A loose limb reached out and gentle fingertips grazed the back of my arm.

I turned half an inch to look back and was thrown four metres.

"Call an ambulance!" A voice to my right said. To my left, those same gentle fingers touched my arm, turning me over. "Don't move her," the same commanding voice spoke quickly.

"I had the light," another voice said. The man who hit me. I didn't know if he was right, I hadn't been paying much attention.

My hip felt like it had been hammered with a log. I'd cracked my head on the asphalt, but I'd hit it harder on the ice. I'd had way worse falls than this. I was okay. I wanted to tell them but all I could do was cry, finally letting out the heaving sobs that had been begging to be released. The physical pain felt like the perfect excuse. I opened my eyes enough to see an older woman, greying and kind-eyed whose hands felt gentle to the touch. I couldn't stop myself from turning to her, crying loudly, brutally. She took me in, holding me softly. "It's okay," she said, "You're going to be okay."

I didn't believe her. But I let myself sink into her. I let myself float away for a little while.

CHAPTER ONE:
The Night We Met
(Six weeks earlier)

BRADY

I hated being home. I hated that the cold and empty Hollywood Hills house was now my home. I spent most of my free days riding my motorbike, letting the roar of the engine drown out my thoughts. I missed my family. I even missed Cat. Though, if I were being honest with myself, not nearly as much as I thought I would.

I rode all across Los Angeles. I rode out to the desert. Joshua Tree. Death Valley. I didn't have any work to keep me busy like I had during the six months after the separation. Now I was free as a bird. For a few weeks at least. Most of my friends were off working. Gregory was busy with his new wife, Malia, and their twin daughters. Laura was doing a play, David was directing his latest film, Ed was midway through acting in a war epic. Everyone was busy. They knew about the breakup, though the public didn't yet. They'd offered me their sympathy. I needed something more than that. I needed a distraction. I needed to get laid.

My phone vibrated in my pocket. I slowed down to a stop and took a look. My manager, Cynthia, wanted to know if I was going tonight. I'd forgotten. Raina, another actress friend of mine, had invited me a few weeks ago to the opening party of this new restaurant and bar that she and her husband had invested in. She said there'd be friends there from the industry, so I'd told her I'd go. I was sure I'd be fine by then. I hadn't been out much since my wife of twelve years had kicked me out of the house we'd shared with our three kids. Maybe this was just the time. Maybe I'd meet someone who would scratch that itch. Or maybe I'd feel worse than I already did. It didn't seem likely.

I texted her back that I'd be there and rode home to get ready. I took a lengthy shower letting the scalding water soothe the aches I'd been nursing since my early morning gym session. After hopping out and towelling myself dry, I looked at myself in the mirror. This was 45, I thought. My dirty blonde hair was slightly thinner. I had new wrinkles around my pale blue eyes, a few lines on my forehead. At least I'd kept fit. I was lean and strong. I thought I might've been in the best shape of my life. Spending half your time in the gym to stay away from your raging wife would do that to you. I still had my six pack and the v line that I was so famous for.

Should I shave? I touched my chin. My hair was short, a little messy from my loose curls, with a few greys. It'd do. I changed into a pair of grey trousers and a grey button down. I put on some black dress shoes and organized a car to take me to the event.

HAVEN

"I don't want to go!" I whined. I'd already agreed. I'd already drank the required amount of pre-drinking alcohol that my best friend and roommate Odessa had laid out for me. I was tipsy. But it wasn't the good kind. It was the kind that reminded me how sad I was that my boyfriend of the last four months had dumped me for gaining a few extra pounds. Even if it was for work. I'd always been a little too curvy for the industry as a model. But a few more pounds, my agent assured me, would put me on top of the plus size modeling industry. If it meant I got to eat dessert now and then, I was all for it. Theo, however, was not. In his words, "I can't be seen dating a fat chick."

Not that we were ever seen. In our short courtship, we dined privately and traveled privately. We were never ever caught by the paparazzi who often tailed him. It didn't bother me that he wanted to keep his private life private. It did bother me that he wanted to control how I looked for the day it would become less private.

"We're going," Odessa said, pulling me up off the couch. "You look so good. It's gonna be so much fun. You can meet someone to take your mind off Theo."

"I don't want to meet anybody," I argued. "I want to stay home and watch Netflix."

"And waste this good buzz?" she asked. "My agent got both of us on the list for this thing. It's too late to change it. I am not going alone. Get your ass ready!" Odessa was a budding actress with gorgeous black skin and a beautifully shaped shaved head. She had talent and she worked hard but she needed the luck-meets-opportunity part of the equation. She was a friend from back home in Alaska and we just so happened to be moving to LA at the same time a year or so ago when I was moving there from New York. Rooming together seemed the reasonable thing to do. She quickly became the best friend I'd ever had.

I groaned. She was right. I was being selfish. I needed to snap out of it. Theo didn't deserve my sadness. He was an asshole. I knew I shouldn't date a guy who's last hundred girlfriends were skinny blondes. But he'd asked. I was beyond flattered. He starred in so many of my favorite movies when I was growing up. I had his posters on my wall. How could I say no? Well I regretted it now, didn't I?

"Okay," I said, rising, shaking off the melancholy and making sure I hadn't messed up my black beaded mini dress with spillage or creasing. I was good. "Let's go."

"Are you sure?" Odessa asked. As annoyed as she'd be if I bailed, she didn't want to be a bad friend and force me out when I wasn't ready. I didn't want to be a bad friend either and bail at the last minute. She needed to network. I needed to leave the house. I nodded. "Let's go."

BRADY

In a quiet corner of the bar, I stood drinking a glass of scotch on the rocks. I decided it was the only thing in that room worth my time. I'd spoken to the few people I could stand, a couple of fellow actors and a director I'd worked with before. I'd scanned the room for someone who could help take my mind off my impending divorce and lasting misery and found nothing that held my interest. Another sweep of the room brought my eyes to the huge metal clock on the wall across from me. I realized it had been an hour and a half; a perfectly acceptable amount of time to spend there. I looked for Raina to say goodbye. Then I lost my breath.

Jesus Christ.

Who the hell is that? I thought as I ran my eyes over her. She was tall, only a couple of inches shorter than me. Curves for fucking days. Long luscious dark brown hair pinned back away from her seriously pretty face. She had big pouty lips, the lower of which was currently trapped between her teeth.

She's young, I thought. But sexy as hell. My cock throbbed within seconds of looking at those eyes. I couldn't see what color they were. She was too far away. But they were piercing. She caught me looking. I looked away.

Not smart. Really not fucking smart. You came to this party to find someone to fuck and she was not the one. She can't have been more than 22. I was probably double her age. But that body. In Hollywood, a girl with some flesh on her bones was harder to find than a cocaine-free surface. Who was she, I wondered? An actress? A model? She had to be something like that. She was too pretty to be a nobody.

HAVEN

Brady Witter. Brady fucking Witter. He was looking right at me. Why the hell was he looking at me? We were in a room filled with Los Angeles' most beautiful women and *the* movie star of our generation, Brady fucking Witter, was looking at me. And, looking embarrassed to have been caught in the act. And yet, he looked at me again.

"Odessa?" I asked. She was chatting with another actress from her agency. "Odessa!" I pressed.

She turned to me, annoyed. "What?" she hissed.

"Is he looking at me?"

Odessa looked around, confused. I watched the confusion turn to shock as her eyes widened and jaw dropped. "Is that Brady Witter?"

"Yes, is he looking?" I asked.

"He was," she answered. "He just looked again," she said excitedly.

I turned back and he was still looking. He smiled a little. I smiled back. I turned back to Odessa. "Oh my god."

"You have all the fucking luck!" she said, referring to the lothario who'd just brutally dumped me, I begged to differ. "Go over there," she said.

"Are you insane? I can't just go approach Brady Witter."

"Why the hell not?" she asked. "I'll do it." I shook my head.

She was always much braver than me. That must've been the actress in her. She could do anything if she was pretending to be someone else. She probably would've approached Theo if he hadn't sent his security over to bring me into the VIP section of the club the night we met.

"No," I said, shaking my head. I glanced back at him. He was chatting with Raina Robertson, America's Sweetheart. Of course, he was. No way could I go over there and interrupt the two of them.

BRADY

I could barely follow along with what Raina was saying. She'd come up to me spouting something about drama with the head chef. I just nodded, looking intermittently over at the beautiful girl. She had been doing the same to me. No way could I approach a girl that age. That would be too creepy. Raina excused herself as Rhys, an old acting school buddy of mine, came to say hello. "How are you?" he asked as he shook my hand. "What have you been up to?"

I rattled on about nothing particular. He'd heard about the projects I had coming up. He told me about his. I asked about his kids and he asked about mine. And, Cat. I reluctantly told him that we were over. "Sorry, man. That sucks."

I nodded. I looked back over to the girl. He followed my gaze. Shit.

"You looking at Haven Roser?" he asked.

"Who?" I asked.

"Haven Roser," he answered. "The model? Long dark hair. Massive tits." They weren't massive. They were proportional to her body. Cat didn't have a lot of shape. She was elegantly long; long legs, long arms, straight. I'd loved her body, but I missed curves.

"Never heard of her," I answered, hoping he wouldn't go on.

"She's dating Theo," he said. "Ah. There he is."

I looked over to see Theo DiGiovanni, an actor whose career had run parallel to mine, in his usual newsboy cap, approaching her where she sat with a few other girls. He never did have a problem dating the young ones. Damn.

"Not his usual type but I'd fuck her," Rhys went on. Sure. As if she'd let him near her. He was as arrogant as they came. I struggled to remember why we'd been friends as he went on about his latest conquests. I looked around the room for other women. I still had an itch that needed scratching. But I couldn't tear my eyes away from her. Haven.

HAVEN

What the fuck? Why is he here? I swallowed as he walked right over to me. "Haven," he said, a question on his lips.

"Theo," I said back. I looked over him, trying to remember why I was so attracted to him. He barely resembled the heartthrob on my childhood bedroom walls. But his green eyes were beautiful. They were so much a part of the charm.

He asked me a question but I could barely hear him. I stood up. "What are you doing here?" he repeated.

"I'm having a drink..." I answered, showing him my half empty glass.

He smiled flatly. "This isn't really your scene."

I furrowed my brows. "What does that mean?"

"It's an industry party," he continued.

"It's a restaurant opening," I argued. Odessa and her friend were looking up at us then with Odessa shooting Theo a vicious glare. I looked over to Brady, he was watching as well.

"Come here for a sec?" he asked, pulling at my arm, leading us into the corridor to the exit.

I pulled my arm from his grip. He'd never handled me like that before. In the four months we'd spent together he could be a little inattentive, but he'd never manhandled me. Any part of him that was ever sweet to me seemed to have vanished from his personality.

"What?" I asked.

"These are my people. You should go."

I laughed a little. Was he serious? "I was here first," I argued. "You should go."

He scoffed. I saw Brady approaching from behind Theo. He clapped a hand on his shoulder. God, he was even better looking up close. I lost my breath a little. Brady was slightly older than Theo but seemed the younger of the two. Theo's looks were nothing compared to Brady. Not now, not ever. "Theo," he said in greeting.

"Brady," Theo said, the charm switched on. This was the guy that asked me out. Oozing charisma. "How are you?"

"Good," he said, before turning to me. "Hi."

"I hoped I'd see you here. Gaillard told me you're in?" Theo asked. Gaillard Trentino? He was a world-famous director. His movies were fun and violent, and I'd seen them all. Theo and Brady must've been gearing up to work with him.

"I am," Brady answered. He looked like he was waiting to be introduced to me. Theo seemed to have no plans to do that. "I'm Brady," he said, taking the initiative.

I shook his hand. Woah. His hand was warm. His touch was electric. It shot straight through me. I took a breath. "Haven," I said, letting it out. I didn't know if I was keeping myself composed but it didn't feel like it.

"Don't bother," Theo said. "She's no one."

No one. Four months and I was no one. I'd met all his friends as his girlfriend. We'd slept together. We'd gone for a weekend to Mexico together. I was a model with a relative amount of fame in my own right. No one? And he said it in front of Brady fucking Witter. I mustered up the barest of smiles for Brady whose expression was unreadable and walked out the exit. Brady or no Brady, I wasn't going to just stand there and take Theo's shit.

I was so embarrassed. I couldn't go back in there. I took out my phone and sent a text to Odessa: *I had to go. Don't be mad.*

Hers came back quick. *I get it. See you at home x*

I put my phone away as a figure appeared beside me. I turned to find Brady Witter standing inches from me. What was that smell? Was that him? He smelled good. Like the barest amount of an oaky cologne and a touch of whiskey on his breath. "Hi."

"Hi," I said back. It was all I could manage.

"He's a dick," Brady continued, with half a shrug. I smiled. He swallowed, his Adam's apple bobbing. Was he nervous too? "Do you want to go for a drink?" he asked.

Oh my god. Yes. Yes. Fuck yes. Brady Witter? "Yeah," I said, hoping my voice wouldn't betray the sheer joy I was experiencing.

He smiled a little and walked over to the black SUV that seemed to be waiting for him. He held open the back door. "After you."

CHAPTER TWO:
A drink and a dance

HAVEN

We barely spoke on the drive. I was too nervous. Everything I could think of sounded idiotic in my head. He wasn't talking either. This was going to be awkward if neither of us could get our shit together enough to say anything, I thought. He gave the taxi driver an address and I gave him a questioning look. He said he used to go there all the time. The staff knew him. The regulars knew him. No one bothered him. I found it hard to believe. The biggest movie star in the world? People who'd never seen a movie in their life knew Brady Witter. And yet, we walked in there like nobodies.

There was a small bistro-style restaurant on the street side. Past that was a beer garden that felt more Mexican cantina than anything else. There was live music and a couple dozen patrons, half a dozen of them salsa dancing on the dusty makeshift dance floor. No one was anywhere near as dressed up as we were. Brady untucked his grey shirt at some point which made him fit in a little better. There was nothing I could do about my cocktail dress, but I did shake out my hair.

"What do you feel like?" Brady asked.

"A beer and a shot?" I suggested. The confrontation with Theo had sobered me up a little.

"A shot?" he queried. I smiled. He laughed a little before making his way to the bar to place our drink order.

"So… what do you do?"

"I'm a model," I answered.

"How do you like it?" he asked, without reaction. I guessed he already knew what I did.

"I like it," I answered. "How do you like being an actor?"

"It's good. I haven't been acting so much lately. There's a lot of other things I want to do these days."

"Like—"

A waiter arrived with our tray of drinks, interrupting my follow-up question.

"Thanks," Brady said as the waiter left us alone.

I picked up the shot. Brady followed.

We clinked and downed our shots. Tequila. That made sense. It burned a little. I took a sip of the beer to quell it. The tequila worked quickly. Or maybe it was just the action of taking the shot. But I started to relax.

"That got a little weird back there," Brady said. Did he mean the minutes in the ride over? The awkward silences? "You and Theo," he clarified.

Oh. "Yeah," I agreed. "Sorry about that."

"Are you okay?" he asked.

"Yeah," I said, shrugging it off. "It was a little embarrassing," I admitted.

"He's the one that should be embarrassed," Brady said. "You two dated?"

I nodded. "Not for long. Four months."

"What happened?" he asked carefully. "If you don't mind me asking..."

I wondered if I should say. The immediate thought was that it's embarrassing to have been dumped for gaining weight. But then I realized I have absolutely nothing to be ashamed of. "I'm making the transition into plus size modelling, so I've had to gain a little weight. He wasn't really keen on that idea."

"Seriously?" Brady asked, his brows furrowing. "That is fucked."

I shifted a little uncomfortably.

"You have a gorgeous body."

BRADY

What the fuck did I just say? I'd been struggling to talk to her since I asked her to go for a drink. I thought the booze would help. The tequila had made me creepier.

"Sorry," I said.

"Don't be sorry," Haven said, sitting up a little straighter, a lip-bitten smile on her face, her cheeks reddening from the booze or embarrassment.

Her eyes were a darker blue than mine, a dark ocean blue. Her hair was longer than I thought. She undid the pins and shook out her locks at one point, sending her perfumed scent my way. She was so sexy. I wanted her. I couldn't deny it. But... "You can't be much older than my oldest."

She smiled again but didn't answer my implied question. My hope was 27. I could convince myself she was almost 30. My honest guess was 22. I didn't want to know.

"When did it end?" I asked, going back to Theo.

"A while ago," she said, not giving any specifics. "Before we met, I had this idea that he was a womanizer... but I get why all these girls fall for him. He's so charming. Until he's not."

"He's a nice guy. If you're someone he wants to fuck."

"So *not* a nice guy," she argued.

"You're right," I agreed. It's what I'd meant.

I looked up, through the open roof, hoping to see some stars. Nothing. It must've been cloudy. When I looked back at her, she was looking over my body, her eyes lingering on the ink peeking out from where my shirt was unbuttoned over my chest. She looked up and realised I'd caught her. She blushed a little harder.

"Brady!" I turned to see Julio, the bar manager smiling down at me. He held out his hand and I shook it.

"Julio. Good to see you," I said before turning to Haven. "This is Haven."

"Hi," she said and shook his hand.

"Where is Cat?" Julio asked, surely not meaning any harm. Haven shifted again, uncomfortable. Did she know about my marriage? What did it mean if she did and had come here with me?

"Home with the kids," I said, not wanting to go into it with the bar manager. "I'll tell her you said hello."

"Okay. Let me know if I can get you anything, okay?" he asked. I nodded and he made his way.

Haven started drinking her beer, nearly chugging, readying to make her move I guessed.

"We're separated," I admitted.

She swallowed and set down the beer. "I'm sorry." She noticed the ring not present on my ring finger. "Can I ask what happened?"

I'd asked the same of her and Theo. It was only fair. "She ended it. If I'm being honest, I'm not sure it was ever right."

"How come?" she asked, her expression so open, without an ounce of judgment.

I went on, "We got together because we both wanted kids. We wanted a family. And we had a lot of chemistry but I'm not sure I ever knew the real her. The second she decided we were over, she became someone else entirely, this stranger. She was so angry. And, I didn't do anything. I mean, I was drinking a bit, smoking, because she was so obviously unhappy. I was working a lot, producing, to stay out of the house and her way. It just fell apart."

Shut up, Brady. Once I started, I couldn't stop. I didn't know this girl at all, and I was just rambling on, telling her things I wouldn't say to some of my closest friends.

"I shouldn't have said any of that," I admitted.

"I won't say anything. I swear. It's all safe with me," she promised. For some reason I believed it.

"You seem like a trustworthy person," I said. "It's a rare thing here." I hoped she wouldn't prove me wrong.

She smiled. "I'm not from here."

"Where are you from?"

"Alaska," she admitted. "Anchorage."

That was interesting. "What did you do in Alaska?"

Julio had the waiter bring over another round of shots and beers.

"Oh god," she said.

But still, we picked up and did the shots, saluting Julio behind the bar.

She took another sip of her beer, likely to rid her mouth of the taste of tequila. It wasn't sweet or smooth, but it did loosen me up like nothing else. It seemed to loosen her up, too. She had relaxed into her chair. She let herself move as she talked. She let herself look at me the way I was sure I was looking at her. With want.

"I moved to New York when I was 16, to start modeling. Before that I wanted to be an ice skater."

"Really? I love skating. You wanted to skate professionally?" I asked.

"I wanted to be an Olympic-level figure skater," she said. I imagined her in those cute little outfits. The short skirts. Her long shapely legs.

"What happened to that dream?" I asked.

"I broke my ankle on a jump," she admitted with a shrug.

"Damn," I said. The band changed things up, going from lively cantina music to something slower, more sensual. "Were you good?" I asked, a thought in mind.

"I was great," she said, all confidence. She was moving a little to the music, just her head and her waist, so slowly.

"Then you must be able to dance," I said, standing up. I took another gulp of my beer and held out a hand.

"No," she said, shaking her head. "They are very different things."

"I bet you can dance. With a body like that," I said again, not being able to help myself. I wanted to dance with her. I wanted an excuse to run my hands all over her. The way she was looking at me, I was sure she wanted the same.

"You have to stop saying things like that," she said. "I can barely talk around you as it is."

I laughed a little. "You don't need to talk to dance."

She swallowed but didn't take my hand. I moved closer, sliding my hand into hers, and pulling her carefully with me. She followed.

HAVEN

He walked a little way, into the middle of the dance floor. He swayed like a man who knew how to dance. He pulled me close. I wrapped my arms around him as he held me by the waist, moving us to the slow guitar melody and drumbeat. We moved in unison until we were casually grinding on the dance floor. He spun me out and brought me back, my back to him. The way he was using his hips was driving me crazy.

I just let the rest of the world fall away. All my embarrassment left me at some point, too. It was just us, the music, the way our bodies fit together, the way his hands felt roaming my waist, my back, my stomach when he turned me, my hips. The way he felt under my hands. His body was strong and lean, his back broad, his lips full. His jaw could cut glass and his pale blue eyes made me shake.

It started to rain. Just lightly at first. The dancers quickly left the dance floor. There was barely an inch of shelter in the beer garden. We didn't stop dancing.

He lifted my hands, holding my arms up as we ground down and back up. He turned me again running the tip of his nose, his lips, over my shoulder, up my neck. Just kiss me...

Lightning flashed, a strobe lighting us on and off. Yet it felt darker than ever. And, I felt braver. I turned around, brought my hands up to his neck and pulled him in. I licked my lips. He watched the move. And then I kissed him. Just lightly. It might've been my only chance. I wanted it to be good. I parted his lips with mine, taking his lower lip, sucking gently until finally he started kissing me back.

He wrapped both arms around me, pulling me tighter against him. I widened our kiss, meeting his tongue and battling with it for dominance. It felt like kissing a god. I had to keep myself together because his mouth threatened to disintegrate me. I grabbed onto his jaw as I took a breath, that perfect sharp edge. I kissed along the line and down to that perfect spot where jaw meets neck. I grabbed the lapels of his shirt before plunging my hands underneath, running them up his chest, around his neck and down his back.

"Fuck," he said, as I sucked at the base of his neck. He grabbed my chin and brought my lips back to him, delving deeper, kissing harder.

Thunder roared! We suddenly looked around, noticing we were all alone out there. No one on the dance floor, no one in the beer garden. And, I wanted him closer, I wanted every part of him closer.

I looked around for the closest chair. I pushed him back to sit and climbed onto his lap. I brought his mouth back to mine and ground into his lap. He grabbed my thighs, shifting himself up, pressing against me, hardening. I groaned.

"Where can we go?" I asked, as his lips roamed my own neck, his fingers pushed up my dress, exploring the skin of my upper thighs. "Brady?" I reminded him of my question.

"How old are you?" he asked. "I've got to know."

Shit. No, I thought. He won't like it. Just lie, I told myself. But I couldn't. "22," I admitted. And, just like that, he stopped sucking on my neck. His hands fell away. Fuck. But he was still hard. He couldn't hide that while I was still grinding on him. "I'm legal," I said, my voice almost pleading.

"I can't," he said, his voice straining.

"Please," I said. "Take me home."

He groaned a little, putting his hands on my hips to still me. I wouldn't let him.

"Take me home," I said again, licking at his lips to open them back up to me. He shook his head. He pushed a little at my hips, he wanted me off. But he didn't. Still, I got up.

He leaned forward, rubbing his fingers on his lips, it was a gesture I'd seen in his films. Concern. I ached for him. I should've lied.

BRADY

I walked with her out to the street. She was soaked from the rain. I wanted to offer her my jacket, but it was just as soaked and wouldn't have helped. She looked embarrassed. I hated that. I felt embarrassed, too. I wanted her. But she was 22, just as I had guessed. It felt so wrong. I couldn't bring myself to do it. Even if the sound of her pleading almost did me in.

I hailed a taxi, held the door for her and said goodbye. She looked at me a few moments, almost as if she was giving me a chance to change my mind. I didn't. She leaned in and kissed my cheek, lingering there like some devil on my shoulder. I closed my eyes letting myself feel the impression of her lips, take in the scent and try and memorize it. Then, within seconds, she was gone.

CHAPTER THREE:
Closer

HAVEN

The next day, his separation was all over the news. That was bound to happen. The breakup before that, when his fiancé had left him days before their wedding, was still brought up regularly.

There was some mention in the articles of a girl in a bar, but no notion of who she was, no pictures. I guessed it was me, though I knew I wasn't the only girl to ever go into a bar, and certainly not with Brady Witter. I quickly circumnavigated the separation news to cyberstalk the other areas of Brady's life.

There were the things I knew, or sort of knew. He and Catalina had three kids. He likes to ride bikes, he's philanthropic, political, a humanitarian. Then the things I didn't. That his real name is William Brady Witter. He was born in St. Louis. His mother died young.

I started watching his interviews. Older and newer. I couldn't help but be struck by how gentle he was, in interviews and in person. An obviously kind person. And, so goddamn good looking.

He's pretty, objectively, with soulful eyes, and those lips that kissed so well. He's had a million different haircuts and facial hair styles. I liked the current short crop, the barest curl to it, and just a dusting of facial hair.

God, I regretted not trying harder to get him to take me home. I knew he wanted to. I could feel it. I wasn't sure what he was afraid of. Actually, I was pretty sure I knew. But what's in an age?

I remembered how he tasted, how he smelled. I remembered what his hands felt like on me. I tried to mimic his touch, but it was futile.

Then another piece of news that I couldn't ignore; the house where he'd gone to live after the breakup with Catalina had been photographed. I recognized it. I didn't know the address, but I knew that I'd walked past it before, I'd done a photoshoot a few doors down from it only weeks before. I opened Google maps and navigated the streets until I found it. I had the address in front of my eyes. Maybe it was insane. Maybe my desire for him, intense as it was, had taken over my mental faculties cause all too suddenly I was showering, changing, ordering myself an Uber and driving to that very spot.

Confidence, I told myself. Stand a little straighter. Slow your breathing. My hands were shaking as I reached over to press the bell beside the gate. Would he even answer himself? Would it be some butler to tell me to get lost? It was too late. The Uber was gone. I was there. I had to just press it.

I pressed the button. It buzzed quietly. I waited a few moments. No answer. Should I leave? No, Haven, try again. I pressed again. Quickly after that, I heard a "hello?"

"Hi..." I wasn't sure who it was. The voice was muffled. It could've been Brady, but it also could have been anyone. "This is Haven..."

"Haven?" the voice repeated. The way he said my name, I knew it was him.

"I'm sorry. I know this is embarrassing. I'll leave if you want me to," I said. "But if you want me half as much as I want you, then let me in."

There was a pause. Just a few seconds. Then another buzz. The gate opened just a little. He didn't say anything more. I opened it further, let myself in and closed it again.

There was a short driveway on a bit of a hill which I climbed carefully in my heels. The house itself was modest. Maybe just three bedrooms.

I reached the door and it swung open. Wow. He was beautiful. A California God in jeans and a t-shirt. And, I was a stalker. All that confidence just evaporated.

BRADY

"Let me in," she said. Her voice was so commanding. Where'd she get that power from? I let her in. I had no intention of giving her what she wanted. Giving myself what I wanted. What I'd been wanting all day. All the night before too, to be honest. I let out a nervous breath as I rushed to the front door. I opened it before she could knock.

She stood there in front of me in fishnet covered legs, black pointed heels, a tan trench coat and god knows what underneath it. She was every bit as beautiful as I remembered. But she'd scrubbed all that makeup off. Her hair was down. She had that undone natural cool, natural beauty like Carolyn Bessette, mixed with this old Hollywood beauty and sex appeal like Marilyn, Liz Taylor, Jean Harlow... It was a breathtaking combination. My intentions were worth shit.

"Hi," I said, leaning against the doorway, trying to be just as cool. It was hard to be cool with bare feet.

"Hi," she said back, her voice had lost all of that confidence I'd heard over the gate speaker. She smiled, nervous. The red in her cheeks only made her more beautiful and every second I kept my eyes on her, I wanted her more. I'd spent enough hours regretting not having her.

"Come in," I said, opening the door wider.

"Thank you." She took her handbag off her shoulder and sat it on the entryway table.

"Can I take your coat?" I asked, reaching for the tan trench coat.

She gripped it tightly. "No, I'm okay. For now. Thanks."

We walked a little further into the house. She looked around, appraising the place. I wished I'd let a decorator have at it. It was still too sparsely furnished. I didn't bring a lot of things with me. It was cold and empty and depressing.

We made it to the kitchen. She looked out past the sunken living room into the backyard. "Would you like a drink?" I asked, reaching for a few glasses.

"Sure," she said. "Whatever you're having."

I poured us two whiskeys, threw in a couple pieces of ice and joined her in the middle of the room. As she took the glass from me, I realized I probably shouldn't be plying her with alcohol. But by then it was too late.

"Thanks," she said, before taking a warm sip. I followed her lead. She twitched her lips a little, not from the whiskey but the awkwardness, I guessed. I had to take the lead here. She'd already come to me.

"Want a tour?" I asked. The place wasn't huge but there was more to see than this.

"Okay," she said, nodding. She finished her drink and set the glass down on the kitchen bench. I kept mine with me, sipping, glad to have something in my hands.

I showed her the kids' bedrooms, already made up with bunks and toys, Mannix's room was slightly more suited to a sixteen-year-old.

I showed her the upstairs living room, a couch and a TV. I couldn't bear how unimpressive it all was. But she was surprised by the size of the place. Looking at it from outside, it did seem modest. I showed her the upstairs bathroom, the clawfoot tub with something of a view. And, then we were at my room. We didn't linger at the door like the other spaces, Haven walked right in, she'd come for a reason.

I was happier with this room more than any of the others. It was more homely, lived in. It contained my books, my scripts, some of my art, my record player and all of my records.

"Who are you listening to?" she asked, looking at my collection.

"A little of everything. Frank Ocean, Radiohead..."

"You have an Alexa," she said, pointing out the device on my bedside. "You're not worried Amazon is recording your conversations?"

I laughed. Was she a conspiracy theorist? She smiled; it was a joke. "I know Jeff Bezos," I answered. "He wouldn't dare."

She nodded with a smile, but her expression turned serious again. She gripped her trench coat, tightening the tie around her waist as she moved toward the window looking out over the city.

Maybe this wasn't it, I thought. The right moment. "We don't have to do anything," I said. "We could go out to eat if you want."

"No," she said quickly, turning her eyes to me. "I want this. I just lost all confidence the second I saw you again."

I scoffed a little. "You lost confidence? I'm the old man here."

"You're the sexiest man alive," she said.

"Two-time sexiest man alive," I teasingly corrected her. Truth be told, I thought the whole sexiest man/beautiful people list thing was bullshit.

She laughed again. "Exactly."

"That was a decade ago," I reminded her.

"Fucking men," she seethed. "You just get better with age."

"I feel like a pervert. You're so young."

"Inexperienced," she said, her cheeks colouring. She bit her lip. They were so pink. So full.

"I really want to kiss you," I said, watching as her teeth let go of her lip.

"I want that, too," she said.

That was all I needed. I took the three steps between us, gripped her cheeks and kissed her. Just as I remembered. Like electricity. I warmed immediately. She opened her lips to me, and I kissed her deeper, basking in the quiet moans that escaped her.

Catalina's lips were too big. She didn't really know how to use them. Haven knows how to kiss. God, I wanna touch her.

HAVEN

I grabbed his waist, running my hands up his hardened abs before they landed on his long thick neck. I pulled him closer.

He moved his hands to my back, running down and over my ass to my thighs. He ran his fingers up the pattern of my fishnet stockings, pushing up my trench coat as they made their way past the stocking to the strip of suspender and then my bare ass. His hands fell away too quickly. His lips left me too. He was looking at me with something like confusion.

"Are you wearing anything underneath that?" he asked, peering into the cleavage just visible in the shadow beneath my trench coat.

"Yeah," I said. "I'm wearing something."

"What?" he asked, sort of desperately. "What are you wearing?

The way he was talking, the way he was looking at me, I was overheating, ready to take it off, my confidence returning in spades. I put my hands on his chest and pushed him backwards until he was sitting on the ottoman at the end of his bed. I took a few steps away and grabbed the tie at my waist. Brady leaned back on his elbows and brought one hand up to rub his chin. His chest rose and fell with his breaths.

I undid the tie and then one button at a time until the coat was open. I dropped it to the floor. I stood for a moment there in front of him, heels, fishnets, suspenders, G-string, demi cup bra and nothing else. His eyes travelled over me. His breathing quickened. He leaned forward but I could still see him hardening.

"What do you think?" I asked, lifting my long hair and dropping it back down. Brady leaned back again and grabbed at his cock in his pants, like he couldn't not.

"Come here," he demanded. I'd been ordered about before, but suddenly it was major turn on. Everything was sexier coming from him. I did as I was told, and he seemed to like it.

He reached up and touched my thighs, gently, like I was some kind of statue to be carefully worshipped. He ran his fingers up my stomach, cupping my breasts before turning me around. He was appraising me. He whispered an expletive as he touched my ass and then turned me around again. I was breathing just as heavily as he was then. I was getting wet where a dull ache was starting to build between my thighs. I wanted him to touch me there. I wanted him to be just as naked as I was.

I reached out and grabbed the first button of his shirt, undoing it. I got down onto my knees as I undid the rest of them and pushed the shirt off him. Yep, a six pack. My god. And, tattoos, all over him. I didn't know that before. They were gorgeous. Nothing gaudy or crazy. Only black. Lots of script and line work. A line art tornado on his waist. I ran my fingers over it, lightly. Then I grabbed his belt.

He grabbed my hands. "Wait."

"What?" I asked.

"Are you sure?"

I rubbed my hand over where he was straining against his jeans, giving him my answer. He groaned. I went back to his belt. Brady's hands dropped; the fight leaving him.

"Fuck it," he said, leaning back, letting me undo his belt and his pants. I took out his long hard cock, another beautiful part of him, and gripped him tightly. I reached between my legs and gathered the wetness there bringing it back using it as a lubricant as I rubbed and squeezed and played.

"Fuck..." Brady groaned. "Haven..."

I wanted to put my mouth on him, but he grabbed my arms and lifted us both up, dropping his pants and then his briefs as he kissed me. His hands went straight back to my ass, squeezing tightly before his fingers found my lace covered cunt. He rubbed, feeling the dampness there before shifting the material and exploring my bare soaked skin. He kissed and sucked at my neck as he did. I grabbed onto him, holding tightly as his ministrations started to take their effect. My legs were losing strength as he put a finger inside me curling it, rubbing his thumb against my clit at the same time.

Then suddenly he was on his knees and his mouth was on me. I almost dropped. But his strong hands held me steady as his tongue went to work on my dripping pussy. I moaned shakily. I held onto his head, running my fingers through his slightly curled locks, rubbing his neck as he worked me over. My moans grew louder as his lapping shot pleasure to every nerve ending of my body.

"Come for me, Haven," he said, and those four words sent me over the edge, shockwaves rippling through me from my core. As I fell apart, he stood while keeping a hand on me. He kept rubbing me gently as he turned us both, so my back was to the bed, and pushed me down. I fell easily and found the energy to drag my way up the bed. I tried to kick off my heels, but Brady reached out. "Leave them," he said.

I spread my legs as he climbed onto the bed, coming between my thighs, the hard length of him straining toward me. I reached down for it, as his hands went to my breasts, pulling them out of their demi cups, fondling, kissing, sucking. "You're so beautiful," he said.

I bucked my hips a little, rubbing myself along the length of him. "So are you," I answered, in a barely-there voice. He let out a shaky breath.

"What do you want?" he asked. He knew, he just wanted me to say it.

I wanted his cock. And, I didn't want to wait for it. We could go back to foreplay after I knew what it felt like to have him inside me.

"Fuck me, Brady," I said, rubbing the head of his cock against my opening.

He groaned a little, more warring inside his head. No, I thought, no more warring. I grabbed his jaw and brought his ice blue eyes back to mine. I looked at him insistent. "Fuck me now," I demanded.

He nodded, finally, and shifted over me, reaching for the drawer of his bedside table. I undid my bra beneath him and tossed it aside. Brady looked over my bare breasts as he slid the condom on. He pumped himself a few times before bringing himself back down to me. I pushed at my lace panties, trying to get them off but the suspenders kept them on. Brady shifted them aside again, but it wasn't enough. "Rip them," I plead. "Fucking rip them."

"Really?" he asked.

I nodded, desperately.

He grabbed them with both hands, ripping them quickly and pulling them away. The air hit my pulsing cunt and I grabbed at his cock, ready for it. We lined up and then looked into each other's eyes. His eyes were so clear, so unyielding. His right eye had the littlest bit of brown surrounding the pupil. I reached down, grabbing at his firm ass, pulling him just enough to get him to make the move and push into me.

I cried out a little, with no fear of being loud. The house was empty. It was just us. He groaned before letting out a "Holy fuck."

We fit together perfectly. My eyes rolled back into my head with the fucking goodness of it.

I wrapped my legs around him. I moved my hands back to his neck, bringing his skin back to me, I wanted to taste him. I licked and sucked at the skin of his neck before he started moving again, just slowly. I felt myself stretch around him as his arms made a cage around me. His forearms strained, the veins appearing over his muscles.

Fuck... had sex ever felt this good? Was it because it was Brady Witter? Was it because it was a man with two decades, almost three, of experience? But Theo had the same and it was never like this. This felt next-level good, like every fuck before it wasn't the real thing.

But he was holding back. Trying to be careful with me, I thought. He didn't need to. As I opened my mouth to tell him he could go faster, he started to speed up. He didn't need me to tell him. He kept one arm by my head, keeping his weight off me, as the other came under me, pulling me closer to him from the base of my back, bringing me up at the hips. It was just the right angle. I kept one arm down to stay steady and ran the other through his dirty blonde hair, feeling the back of his neck, and gripping the short locks there.

I already felt that good tightness, that torturous coiling all over again. I wanted to come. But I didn't want it to ever be over.

BRADY

I brought her legs up, making more room for myself. She felt so tight. So warm. So. Fucking. Good. The push and pull as she milked my cock, as I stretched her out, as we moved together, touched, kissed, sucked, over and over, desirous and delirious... Nothing had ever felt so good. First that fucking performance. I'd seen plenty of beautiful women take off their clothes. But nothing had ever turned me on like Haven dropping her trench coat to reveal her slinky black lingerie and suspenders. Then the way she spoke, the way she asked for exactly what she wanted and how I knew it exactly. She was the most perfect thing I'd ever seen or fucked. Fuck my life, right?

It was going too quick. I was going to come. She had to come first. I reached down and pressed on her clit. She cried out a little breathy. I gave her two fingers, playing her like an instrument. She threw her arms back, reaching for my headboard, her breasts bounced beneath me. I bent over and sucked at her nipples, flicking them with my tongue, biting at one of them. I wanted to mark her. I wanted her to be mine.

Her body jerked and shuddered beneath me as she came again. She let out groans and moans, expletives, my name, over and over, no restraint, no shame. I came next, with my own shudder, my own loud moan, into her ear, as she gyrated slowly, basking in her orgasm.

I let myself fall onto her. Both of us were covered in a sheen of sweat, our bodies hot and fatigued. She whispered something I couldn't hear but I felt her hot breath in my ear. I'd given in. And, it was fucking incredible. What the fuck do I do now?

CHAPTER FOUR: Can I kiss you one more time?

HAVEN

We lay like that, recovering for a few minutes before he shifted away from me to get rid of the condom. I thought he'd come back. I thought he'd wrap me in his arms, but he didn't. I got up then, used his en suite bathroom, put my clothes back on and went in search of him.

He was sitting on his lounge, in his boxers, his head in his hands. Was it really that much of a problem?

"You're such a drama queen," I said with a laugh.

"This isn't funny, Haven," he said.

"I'm a grown woman, Brady." I stood there staring at him.

"I know," he said but I knew he didn't.

"What happens now then?" I asked.

"Let me change and I'll drive you home," he said, standing up.

"Can I see you again?" I asked, trying to suppress the desperation.

He ran an anxious hand through his hair. "I don't think that's a good idea."

"Why?" I asked, simply. I knew the answer.

"It just can't happen," Brady said.

"It already happened," I reminded him, smiling at the thought of it.

Brady smiled a little too. "It can't happen again."

My smile faded. "Cause of my age? Or something else?"

"You're too young for me, Haven," he said, walking toward me.

"I'm an adult," I answered, wishing it didn't sound so childish.

"I know that," he said. He passed me by with a touch of my arm. "Let me change. I'll drive you home."

"I can get an Uber," I assured him, feeling beyond frustrated.

"I'll drive you," he answered, walking into his bedroom.

I huffed a little and sat down. I'd just had the best sex of my life and I was being thrown out. Maybe it wasn't so great for him. He'd been with tons of women. Older, more beautiful, more experienced. But how could it have been that good for me and not that good for him? God, that sucked. I wanted to do it over and over again. And obviously he... didn't.

I must've been looking kind of pitiful when he came back out, changed into Chelsea boots, black jeans and a black t-shirt, because he smiled at me, a genuine smile, like he wanted to make me smile back. Of course, I did. I couldn't imagine refusing him anything he wanted.

"You ready?" He asked.

No. I nodded.

He drove me home in a black Tesla, the windows so darkly tinted that I could barely see outside them. There was an unending silence. There felt like so little to say after everything that had already been said. We wanted each other. He wasn't going to let anything more happen. That was that.

"Is this new?" I asked, trying desperately to make conversation.

"About a year," he said.

"I've always wanted a Tesla."

"Do you have a car?" He asked.

I shook my head. "I never needed one in New York and I just never thought of it out here."

"New York is a little different," he said.

I nodded. "This right," I said, directing him.

"This one?" He asked, sounding surprised as we pulled up.

"Yeah," I answered, confused. The building was a little historic, but the inside was brand new. It was actually quite an expensive apartment that Odessa and I shared. Was he judging me? "Why?"

"I stay in the Bridges Hotel sometimes, when I've been out in Hollywood can't make it home." And, for other reasons, I guessed. I wasn't the only girl in Los Angeles who wanted to fuck Brady Witter.

"That's convenient," I said with a shy smile.

He parked the car in front of the building. He looked at me for a moment and I took another shot. "So tomorrow?" I joked. "I play a mean game of snooker."

He smiled a little before getting serious. "I meant what I said," he started. "We can't see each other again."

I rolled my eyes. How repetitive.

"I'm serious. I never wanted to be one of these guys. Like Theo, fucking teenagers," he reached into his glove box and took out a packet of cigarettes and a lighter from the compartment in his driver's side door.

He lit up as I made my rebuttal. "I'm not a teenager. And, wasn't it good?" The second sentence was quiet. I had to know.

"It was fucking incredible. It's going to be really fucking hard not to do it again, but it's for the best. This can't go anywhere." I smiled in relief before the rest of it hit me. Never again? That just would not work for me. But I wasn't going to beg and plead. I'd done enough of that already.

"Really? Cause I was hoping you'd marry me," I teased.

He got it. He laughed a little.

I said what I meant. "I do want to fuck you again."

BRADY

"Jesus," I said. Love a girl who says what she means, I thought. But... "There are plenty of guys your age who would be dying to fuck you."

"How do you know that?" Her brows furrowed. She didn't like being told no.

I looked over her again. "I know."

"Well how many of them are going to make me come over and over again? I can answer that for you. None." My cock was already hardening again. Who is this girl?

"They'll get better. Just help them out a little?" It took some time for me to figure out and a few very vocal girlfriends.

"I shouldn't have to do that," she shrugged.

"No, you shouldn't."

She didn't seem to want to get out of the car. She looked off in front of us, at the cars parked, the empty road. She was strong willed for her age, I thought. And funny. And mature. And 22, I reminded myself. Twenty-two. I remembered what I was like at that age. A fucking idiot. I fell in love with every girl I met. Or I thought I did. In the end, I'd only truly loved two women. Both had wrecked me in their own ways. I wondered what it would have been like to meet Haven back then.

"I wish we were born at the same time. Met when I was 22," I mused aloud.

"You wouldn't have noticed me," she brushed her hair over her shoulders.

"I would've," I insisted. "It would've been impossible not to." I knew it to be true.

She smiled; her mouth closed. She licked her lips then, sucking her lower lip into her mouth, gripping it in her teeth. I loved to see her do that. "Can I kiss you one more time?" she asked, staring at my lips the way I was staring at hers.

I looked around us. Plenty of parked cars, all looking empty. The street empty, too. No sign of paps. A Tesla never got any attention in this town.

I put my arm against the head of her seat. I reached my other hand over onto her neck, into her hair, and brought her close. She released that perfect lip and I watched her close her eyes. I kept mine open. I wanted to remember what she looked like in that moment. I leaned in and pressed a kiss to her lips. Any intention I had to leave it at a peck, evaporated as she took a breath, licked at my lips and opened them up to her. She leaned over the centre console, her hands on my neck, her tongue in my mouth, taking everything she wanted. My hands went to her cheeks before moving down to her back, bringing her body closer to mine.

I imagined the car heating up, the windows fogging, and then the horrifying flashing of cameras. We couldn't do this here. We couldn't do this ever again. That was the decision and I had to stick to it. I turned my cheek. I didn't want to look back and see her expression. I heard her shift back into her seat. In my periphery, I saw her wipe her lips. Then she reached for the door. I turned back then.

"Thank you for today," I said.

"Thank you," she said sweetly, sadly. "Bye."

"Bye," I said, as I watched her step out of the car and walk into her building, no wave, no look back. Then she was gone, taking all the new color I had in my life. Back to grey, I thought.

HAVEN

I rode the elevator in a cloud of bliss and despair. Remembering his kiss, what it felt like to be beneath him, wrapped around him, was blissful. Even just talking to him made me happier than anything else had in a long time. The idea that it would never happen again left me desolate.

I walked through the door to find Odessa eating ice cream from the tub on the floor in front of the lounge. Her cheeks were wet with tears that glistened as she tried to smile at me.

"Hi," she said, her mouth full.

"Hi," I said, rushing over to her side. I saw a small mess of ice cream on the floor.

She saw me look at it. "I spilled," she explained.

"What happened?" I asked.

She smiled a little, but it twisted into a frown as fresh tears sprang from her eyes. I put an arm around her, comforting my sad best friend, waiting for her to be ready to speak.

"I didn't get the part," she said.

I knew which part she meant. She'd already had two auditions and a screen test the week before with Etienne Charpentier, a multilingual actor with a face out of a renaissance painting, who recently broke through the industry with an Oscar-nominated performance. He was apparently incredibly sweet in person, and they had incredible chemistry during the read. Odessa had been sure she had it.

"I'm sorry," I said. "They are idiots."

"It's just never going to happen," she cried.

This wasn't the first time I'd found her this way. She'd been trying to make it from Alaska for years, sending audition tapes and meeting people over Skype. She'd come out to Los Angeles because her agents said she needed to be here. She'd come close to booking so many jobs but still, in all her time in LA, she'd never booked a thing. It had to be disheartening. Still, I was jealous of her passion.

"You'll make it, Odessa. You can't not. You're too talented, too vibrant, too watchable. Someone will figure it out. Something's gotta give." I was sure it would. I'd seen her tapes. I'd seen her in local plays. She had the talent. She just didn't have any luck.

"And, if it doesn't?" She asked me, with a hopeless expression.

I grabbed the spoon and ice cream, taking a big scoop for myself. "You can become my sugar baby," I answered, my mouth full, hoping and succeeding in making her smile.

"Okay," she said. "No funny stuff."

"Just cuddles," I answered, giving her back the ice cream and pulling her closer.

She turned more toward me and hugging me back tightly. "It's going to happen, Odessa," I whispered in her ear. "I know it."

"Thank you," she said back.

BRADY

I had costume and camera tests the next day. They made a welcome respite from the all-consuming thoughts of Haven. Haven's perfectly round breasts. Haven's long curly hair brushing over me. Her hands on my skin, my dick. Her lips.

"Brady!" Theo entered the makeup room with a wide smile. "How's it going?"

He came over and shook my hand. "Yeah good. How you been?"

"Good. Good." He took his seat. His hair stylist approached and started working. "It was nice seeing you the other night," he continued.

"Yeah, you too."

"What did you think of Haven?" He asked, throwing his feet clad in dirty Vans up on the bench in front of him.

I swallowed. "Who?"

"The brunette. I was talking to her when you came up..."

"Right," I nodded. "Seemed nice."

"She's a sweet girl. Incredible face," he leaned over a little. "Fantastic in bed," he whispered, as if the two women working away behind us couldn't hear.

I nodded to give him some kind of response but not enough to encourage him to keep going. I should have told him to stop.

"A little on the heavy side."

"Heavy?" I asked, anger curling my stomach.

"She was curvy when we met but her agency has told her to put on weight to be a plus size model and she's doing it. I told her she should just lose weight instead..." he ripped open a packet of chips and started gorging himself.

"You dumped her cause she's putting on a little weight?" I asked.

"Why would I date a fat chick?" He asked.

I wanted to clock him. My hands balled into fists. I clenched my teeth. Don't move a muscle, I told myself. Keep calm.

But he just kept talking. "I'm gonna miss that mouth though."

"Stop," I said, quietly, unable to hold it in.

"I wouldn't mind another go, to be honest. Maybe I'll give her a call tonight," he winked at me.

I almost leapt from my chair. My makeup artist put a hand on my shoulder. "Turn around would you please, Brady?" She asked. I took a breath and then turned myself around. She was looking at me seriously. It seemed to say, 'Don't. He's not worth it.' I nodded. She started powdering my face. Then she turned me back around and moved in front of me.

"What do you think?" Theo asked, continuing his train of thought.

"Don't..." I started, my voice filled with anger. I made my tone a little more casual. "Don't talk about her that way."

Theo angled his head a little, squinting a little in surprise. "Come on. I don't mean it like that."

"Like what? Just don't. Show some respect." The hair stylist and makeup artist smiled a little, seeming to agree with me.

"You're right," he said quickly, noticing their reactions. "I'm sorry. Just fucking around."

I just shrugged. It wasn't me needing the apology. But I also didn't want him talking to her, seeing her again.

God, I wished I could call her. I didn't get her number the first time and I'd regretted it. I should've got it the second time, but the responsible side of me got in the way, trying to keep guilty pleasure as far from me as possible. I knew where she lived. I could go there, like she came to my house. I didn't know which unit it was, but I could wait outside for her to come out. No, you fucking psycho. You didn't get her number for a reason, I reminded myself. It doesn't matter how mature she seems. It doesn't matter that she's a fucking great lay. It doesn't matter that you like talking to her, laughing with her, looking at her. She's too young for you. No one in your life would get it. Everyone would judge you. It would send Cat up the fucking wall. Just let it go, I told myself. No damn point to it.

"So, what are you doing tonight?" Theo asked. "There is a club opening—"

I cut him off. "Got plans."

"Ah," he said, bristling a little. I tried to soften. "Seeing my kids. How about another time?"

"You got it," he answered with an easy smile before turning his conversational skills on the hair stylist.

"You're done," my makeup artist said with a tap on my shoulders.

"Thank you," I said, going over the look. My skin was tanned. My hair was put into a wig with hair just above my shoulders and long sideburns. Very 70s. I wondered what Haven would think. Fuck!

CHAPTER FIVE:
Bad Ideas

HAVEN

The wind whipped around my hair, curled tightly around my head like a 50s movie star. My white silk dress was lifting, threatening to reveal my lack of underwear to my co-star and the crew. My arms were covered in goose bumps, but he was perfectly warm in his black and white tux. He held me tightly in his arms, his back against the letter E of the Roosevelt sign.

"Are you okay?" He asked me, feeling my distraction.

"My dress is just flying everywhere."

His hands immediately went to my thighs, holding it down like a gentleman.

"You're not wearing anything underneath, are you?" He said, ruining the illusion.

My co-star was a young male model, very tall, black eyes, bleached blonde hair and a name I had already forgotten.

"They wouldn't allow it," I answered.

"Haven, can you just adjust your dress a little?" The photographer said, gesturing to the neckline of my dress which had gotten a little rolled up. I made the adjustments with the model looking too closely and we got back into our position.

"Larkin," the photographer yelled next. So that was his name. "Can you grab her thigh?"

"May I?" Larkin asked.

I smiled my permission to him and lifted my leg. He caught it and brought it against him.

"I wonder what it would be like to fuck up here," he continued. One gentlemanly remark followed by a creepy one.

"Yeah," I said, focusing on posing rather than chatting. Maybe with his cheekbones, his pouty lips, he didn't need to pose, but my face needed work.

"Okay, just switching lenses," the photographer said, giving us a break. I got my leg back and stepped away, rubbing at my arms.

"You're welcome to some of my body warmth." Larkin opened his jacket up and gestured for me to come in.

"I'm okay," I said.

"Come on, don't be silly. It's freezing up here." That was true. And I already had to be all over him. Why not get the benefit of heat too?

I walked into his arms and he wrapped the jacket around me.

"How's that?" He asked.

"Good," I said, honestly, feeling the warmth of his body immediately warming mine. I felt the goose bumps going away.

"That's good," he said. "You and I should go out tonight."

You and I should go out tonight? Not 'would you like to go out tonight?' or 'Can I take you to dinner?' Clumsy pick up.

"I'm seeing someone," I answered.

"So what?" He asked, a cocky smile on his face.

"So no," I said, a wide smile on mine.

"You're a bit of a tease, aren't you?" He asked, seeming to decide I was some kind of challenge.

"Not really," I answered.

He opened his arms as he noticed the photographer get back in place, new lens on the camera and a new sense of purpose. "Haven, we'll have you against the letter and Larkin leaning into her."

We took our new positions. I grabbed onto his lapels and brought him in. He smiled, staring down at my lips.

"I think by the end of today, you'll be agreeing to go out with me. And, by the end of the night I'll have you in my bed."

It was so ridiculous, I had to laugh. I was glad he didn't get angry about it. He just smiled, darkly.

"You'll see."

He kept that same dark cocky smile for the rest of the shoot. When I walked out of hair and makeup with a quick "see ya 'round" I wished I could've seen it drop.

At the end of the night, I had myself tucked under my lavender Egyptian cotton sheets, giving myself a much better orgasm than could ever be achieved by this Larkin, but sadly nowhere close to as good as the ones Brady had given me.

It was tragic to get something so good, so young. It set too high a standard. I couldn't let him keep his word. I wouldn't let the night before be the last time I had him. Not if I could help it.

BRADY

My eldest, Mannix, didn't come to visit me. Truthfully, I hadn't expected him to. Before my wife had kicked me out, it had seemed to me like my son had chosen a side. He didn't appreciate my drinking either. I tried not to think about how sad that made me. That he'd noticed it. I focused on my daughters, sitting on opposite sides of the table, eating a feast of roast pork and vegetables.

They were the reason I couldn't regret my time with Cat. They were such beautiful kids. Inside and out. She was a great mother. Like mine was before she passed. And, I had always wanted to be a father. A good father. A present father. I hated the thought that I would only get to spend a limited amount of time with them. I hated that I wouldn't be able to be there for everything. I promised myself I would do everything possible to spend as much as time with them as I would've if their mother and I had stayed together.

I wondered what they would think of me dating again. Not that they needed to know anything. Not until I was sure of one particular person. And, Haven Roser refused to stay in the recesses of my mind where I continued to shove her. I barely knew her, but I wanted to. I knew it was idiotic, but I couldn't stop my mind from churning. I imagined her in the empty seat of the table. I imagined her beside my youngest daughter, golden-haired seven-year-old, Vera. I wondered what kind of mother she'd be. She probably had no interest in motherhood at her age. It must be the furthest thing from her mind as she was pursuing her career, traveling, partying. But still, I imagined her there. I imagined introducing them to her. I imagined she'd be sweet and loving. She'd never try and take on their mother's duties, only be a support system, a friend. A friend... of course, because she was twenty-fucking-two. Just five years would've helped. Three even. How could one number, two digits, be so threatening?

My phone rang, distracting me from my torturous imaginings. I excused myself from the table and took the phone call in the backyard.

"We got an offer," Cynthia started, as she usually did.

"I'm just with the kids, can you tell me quickly?" I asked.

"Yes. One day shoot. $5 million deal for 3 years exclusive use. A watch company..." she searched for the name. "Patek Phillippe."

"That's interesting," I answered. I liked their watches. There was a Patek Phillippe on my dresser as we spoke.

"The initial campaign is alongside a plus size model..." she added. "Haven Roser."

Are you fucking kidding me? What are the odds? If there is a god, he is utterly against me.

"Do you know her?" Cynthia pressed.

"I met her the other day, strangely." I kicked feebly at the grass that had grown too long. The pool a little further off had started to fill with leaves. Things I didn't have to worry about at home with a household of staff.

"She's a sweetheart apparently. I've seen her pictures. Very pretty."

"Yeah. She is," I agreed, imagining her unflinching blue eyes, her full lips.

"I'll send you an email with the offer. And the link to her portfolio."

"Okay. Thanks."

"Speak soon," she said, her usual sign off.

I hung up and walked back inside.

"How are we doing?" I asked, taking a seat back at the table.

"It's a little dry," my twelve-year-old, Zola, said, apologetically. I wasn't the greatest chef, but I thought it tasted okay. Cat never cooked so the chef would cook most of the time. They were used to perfect meals.

"Is it?" I asked. "Sorry, baby. You want something else?"

"No, it's okay," she said. My middle child was quiet and sensitive. She hadn't let us know much of what she was feeling about the separation.

"We've got dessert next," I said. I was glad I'd bought some pies instead of attempting to make them myself.

My phone beeped with the email. I opened the link straight away, not bothering with the contract. The web page was slow to open. Come on, I thought. Finally, it loaded. There was picture after picture of Haven. Half of them in lingerie. Fuck... I couldn't do this here, I thought. I'd wait until the kids went home. God, I was a glutton for punishment.

HAVEN

A couple of days passed by, none of them without thoughts of him. I couldn't help but internet stalk him. There was just way too much content out there about him. I couldn't control myself. I was so enthralled by the way he carried himself, how he shook every hand, and introduced himself to every person as if they didn't know his name. How he sat back relaxed in every chair, so comfortable in his own skin. How he was always generous and kind, answering every question with consideration, even the ones I would've considered intrusive and rude. He had gentlemanly manners, never interrupting, passing the harder questions to the women working alongside him when sexist interviewers would only pose questions about diet and fashion to them. And god, that smile.

I had a few shoots to keep me occupied during the day, but the night was different. I was itching to go back to that house. Odessa, who had wrenched all the dirty details from me, had appointed herself my warden.

"You're not going," she insisted.

"I know he wants me," I argued as I put on my makeup in the living room mirror.

"You cannot just keep showing up. That's literally stalking." She sat down beside me, taking the eyebrow pencil from my hands. I could do my right brow so easily, but the left eluded me.

"It's not stalking if he lets me in."

"Why don't you try calling?" she asked, finishing my eyebrow off and handing me back the pencil.

"He wouldn't give me his number and he wouldn't take mine," I answered.

"Isn't that some clue then?"

I huffed.

"Listen." She turned me around to face her. "Right now, you've had a really hot hook up and a sweet goodbye. If you show up there and he turns you away, you've ruined that forever."

"But what if he doesn't?" I asked, imagining what it would be like to be under him again or above him, or in the shower with him. I had never been so hungry for anyone before and it was unabating.

"Do you want to take that chance?" I imagined a door slamming in my face. I imagined Brady's face twisted into an expression of pity or even worse, disgust.

Odessa was right. Why tarnish the memory? I needed to busy myself elsewhere.

"Go skating with me?" I asked. I'd bought Odessa her own pair of skates hoping she might be inclined to join me one of these days. She hadn't yet.

"I have an audition to prep for," she answered. "But good idea. Go skating. You might run into someone cute!"

I kept the sexy pink bra and panty set on but changed out the black leather coat dress for a sparkly burnt orange body con mini dress. I tied my hair back and threw on some big gold hoops to complete the look. I put on the skates and rolled my way back into the living room.

"Wow, Haven!" Odessa whistled.

"I didn't want to waste the makeup," I answered, giving a little twirl.

"You will definitely run into someone cute. Or they'll run you down," she teased. I blew her a kiss and made my way out the door. I put on my headphones, lined up the perfect disco tune – Alicia Bridges' *I Love the Nightlife* – before securing my phone in my bra and started skating.

Please don't talk about love tonight
Please don't talk about sweet love
Please don't talk about being true
And all the trouble we've been through

I skated the streets as if I were a 70s roller disco queen with none of the expected self-consciousness. The song wouldn't allow it.

I got to a set of lights and slowed. The car full of young men waiting there, noticed me almost all at once and started hooting and hollering. I wasn't one to enjoy a catcall generally but feeling rejected had turned to feeling hot and I let myself enjoy it.

I crossed the road with a little flare, a turn and a wink to the car, and the hooting became honking and light flashing and I couldn't help but laugh.

The night was warm, and the lights were as beautiful as ever as I glided gently down the Sunset Strip, the wind whipping by me, the disco jams in my ear propelling me forward. My mind fell quiet, finally.

BRADY

Cat sounded terrified. She'd called in a panic. Mannix was supposed to be home by 10, but it was after 12 and he wasn't answering his phone. "He's not with me," I told her. I hadn't seen him since she'd thrown me out. He never answered any of my calls, but I told her I'd try. When he didn't answer, I called her back.

"I'm going to go out looking," she said.

I knew what I was like at his age, just wandering around, getting up to mischief with a couple of friends. He was probably playing video games at someone's house and lost track of time. I was sure he was fine. But I told her I'd go too.

"You don't have to do that," she said.

"He's my son too, Cat," I said.

She let out a breath. "Okay," she agreed. "Call me if—"

"I will," I assured her. I hung up and grabbed my keys, getting into my Tesla and taking off down the driveway.

The night was warm, and the streets were still crawling with people. I drove to the parks I knew he liked. I drove by a few of his friends' houses to see if there were more than a couple cars out front. No one seemed to be having a party. After twenty minutes, Cat sent a text.

Cat: *He's home.*

Brady: *Thanks for letting me know.*

I took a turn to start my way back home, throwing on the radio now that I could relax. It was midway through a song I knew fairly well. Player's *Baby Come Back.*

I focused on the lyrics. *Baby come back, any kind of fool could see... there was something in everything about you.* Was the universe trying to tell me something? If it wanted me to think of Cat, it was failing. The face in my mind's eye was younger, softer, a smile playing on her pink lips, her pretty eyes dancing with laughter. The song ended, transitioning into another classic; *Miss You* by The Rolling Stones. I must've stumbled onto a 70s night and I could've laughed.

I've been holding out so long

I've been sleepin' all alone

Lord, I miss you.

I didn't think it was possible to miss someone you barely knew. But miss her I did. I needed to get her out of my head. I changed the station and Queen's *Somebody to Love* was blasting. That was one too many signs. I shut the damn thing off.

I stopped at a set of lights and watched as a group of young drunk guys stumbled out of a club. A couple of them started play fighting and it made me smile. The group started to separate as a woman in an orange dress approached.

I knew that figure. I knew that hair. She spun around smiling as they seemed to serve up praise. Haven, in a skin-tight shimmering orange dress, her hair pushed back, her long legs tied into white roller skates, skated right by me.

Just keep driving, Brady, I told myself. Take yourself home, jack off in the shower. To a picture of her if you have to. Just leave the real thing the hell alone.

My hands didn't want to listen as I eventually turned my car around and went in search for her. I kept my eyes peeled on each side of the strip; she shouldn't have been too hard to find. Then I realized why I couldn't see her. She was surrounded on all sides by three out of the group of guys who had been cheering her on earlier. They must've followed her.

They were too close, too handsy, their light-hearted cat calling turned into the exact thing women expect it to. My hands tensed on the wheel as I quickly and illegally pulled over.

"Hey!" I shouted out. They turned to see me coming. I tried to keep the fury off my face. Haven turned too. Her mouth dropped.

"Brady Witter! Holy shit!" One of the guys came right over, the stench of beer on his breath. "Can I get a picture?"

"No," I answered, pushing past him and toward the others. One of them was still standing way too close. "Are you okay?" I asked her.

"Better now," she answered, and smiled, pushing the guy who didn't understand the meaning of personal space, further away from her.

"You need a lift?"

"Sure," she nodded. She skated toward me and I led her back to the car, opening the door and closing it behind her as she got in.

The Neanderthals had their phones out, ready to take photos, but we were already driving away.

"Are you okay?" I asked.

She tugged her short dress down her legs, I guessed it wasn't made for sitting. "I'm fine," she said. "They were just being idiots."

"I thought it would be Theo I'd be fighting for your honor," I joked.

"You don't need to fight anyone," she said. "I can handle myself."

I was sure she could.

"I'm glad to see you, though," she said, turning her body to face me.

"Yeah?" I asked. "You do that a lot? Skate on the streets of LA in the middle of the night?" I sounded like her dad.

"It's become a habit."

"You should get rid of it. It's not smart."

"I told you, I can handle myself," she repeated.

"What do I have to do to make you stop? I've lived here most of my life. That situation we just left could've been much worse."

"Okay, daddy," she said, teasingly.

I fucking hated myself for how turned on those two words made me. "I'm serious," I said, trying to hide it.

"Okay," she said, not promising anything. "Where are we going?"

I hadn't thought of that. "Home, I guess."

"Yours or mine?" she asked, her hand reaching over to touch my thigh. This was the girl who charged her way into my house. God, I loved her confidence. I loved how much she wanted me.

But I'd already made a mistake out of her. "I'll drop you home."

She retracted her hand and turned her body with a small huff. That was more like the 22-year-olds I knew. She seemed to go into her own head, having a conversation I wasn't privy to. Then she seemed to change her mind.

She turned toward me, leaned back and rested on the passenger seat door, looking over me with that desirous look I remembered. I was in trouble.

HAVEN

This was my chance. No way was I letting him just drop me at home. After he saved me from a few deadbeats that wouldn't stop following me, not that I would ever give him the credit for that, I was in his car and I had him inches from me. I wanted him more than ever. He looked so good in his loose camel chinos and navy blue shirt. Actually delectable. I kept my gaze on him, trying to figure out my big move, the one that would make him change his mind.

"What?" he asked, his brows furrowed a little, his mouth quirked into half a smile, like he knew my plans.

"Nothing," I said. "Let's get a drink."

He took another look at me before turning back to the road. "I don't think so."

"You're not thirsty?" I asked.

"Nope," he answered, his Adam's apple bobbing in his throat as he swallowed.

"Hungry?" I asked.

He looked back to me, knowingly. "Are you?"

"I am starving," I answered. "For you." Cheesy. I wished I were cleverer.

He slowly shook his head. "Haven..." he started warningly. I took a breath, channeled that 70s disco queen confidence, and I reached under my dress and pulled down my pink lace panties, leaving them on the passenger side floor of his Tesla. "What are you doing?"

I leaned forward, over the console, and took one of his hands off the steering wheel. I brought it toward me, running my thumb up his fingers to straighten them out and then brought them to my lips, kissing the tips of his fingers, kissing down the palm of his hand.

Then I brought his hand, down my chin, my throat, my chest, making a trail along my body until it reached my lap. I started to spread my legs. Brady half-heartedly tried to take his hand back, but I kept it and he let me. Brady wouldn't let himself look as I brought his hand down to feel my bare wet cunt. Finally, he looked, just quickly, and took a hard breath. He put his eyes back on the road, but his fingers went to work, just as I hoped they would. My head rolled back as he rubbed my soft flesh. I grabbed at his forearm.

"This is fucking stupid," he said, looking around at the cars passing us by, his fingers unceasing.

"Then take me somewhere," I said. "I need you, Brady."

BEEP! "Fuck!" Brady slammed on the brakes at a red light he'd almost missed. His hand was gone. I closed my legs, immediately aching for his touch. Brady banged his fists against the steering wheel. "Fuck! What are you doing to me, Haven?" He looked back at me, bewildered but esurient beneath it.

As the car started moving again, I moved forward, reached over and started to undo his pants. His hand came down onto mine. I lifted it off and kissed it again. Brady looked into my eyes.

"It's okay," I told him. His hand moved to caress my cheek and then to my neck as I took his hard-on from his pants, the way I'd been longing to, and brought my mouth down to it, sucking gently at the head as my hands took to his shaft. His fingers wrapped around the back of my neck squeezing as he started to moan. I licked and sucked down the shaft and back up, sucking the precum from the tip before going back down again, wetting the whole thing in my spit, as I jacked him off with my hands.

"So fucking stupid," Brady said breathily. "So fucking good."

I took his entire dick into my mouth, taking him as deep as I could.

I heard him swear above me, his fingers around my neck got tighter. I let go of him and came back up. I kissed along his dick as I spoke. "Brady?"

"Yeah?" he said, just barely.

"I want you to fuck my mouth," I said.

"What?" he said, like he could barely hear me. I turned my face up, my eyes to him, kissing my lips on his cock.

"I want you to fuck my mouth," I said.

His head rolled back. "I'm going to crash this fucking car."

"Don't do that," I said, pressing another kiss to his straining cock. "It's a Tesla, right?"

"Fuck! Wait."

With his grip still on my neck, he pushed me gently away. That was not what I was aiming for. He took his hand and put himself back in his pants. "What are you doing?" I asked.

He didn't answer. He just drove faster.

"Where are we going?" I asked, as he sped through yellow light after yellow light. He drove us up the mountains, down streets I'd never gone before, too fast for me to make out street signs or anything else.

"Brady?" I asked again before he pulled us onto a dirt road and turned off the car. "Where are we?"

"Somewhere we can be alone," he said, before unbuckling his seatbelt.

I smiled, biting my lip, feeling myself turn on at the thought of everything we could do on that quiet dirt road. But first things first. I reached back over, took his cock back out of his pants and went back to work, taking him into my mouth fully. Brady groaned, before reaching down and putting his seat back so he was half laying, and then brought both hands back to my head.

"Jesus." He moved just a little, thrusting his hips along with my bobbing head. "Haven?

I felt him straining, his orgasm building. I licked back up his cock and popped it out of my mouth. "Yeah?"

"I'm going to come," Brady said, half a question in it.

I put my mouth back on him, hollowed my cheeks and sucked.

"Fuck!" He said, he could feel it building. "You want it in your mouth, baby?" he asked.

Baby? I could've fucking died. Yes, god, yes, I wanted him in my mouth. I wanted to taste him, I wanted to swallow him. I wanted to do this every damn day of my damn life.

I nodded as best I could, and finally he came, hot spurting cum ran down my throat like my new favorite dessert and I moaned as I drank it all in, sucking him gently as he let go.

I wiped my mouth a little as I sat back and appraised the man in front of me, spent. My cunt was pulsing. I wanted him inside me. Did it work? I wondered. Did my big move make him change his mind?

He looked over at me, even more bewildered. "Are you trying to ruin me?" he asked.

"Like you've ruined me," I answered. "For anyone but you. Did it work?"

"Maybe," he said. "That was fucking phenomenal."

"Thank you."

"Just gimme a sec," he said, still coming down.

My phone had fallen out, between our seats. It was stuck down there with a chord. I took them both out.

"Play something," Brady said.

I plugged in my phone and chose a song.

"What's this?" he asked.

"Lana Del Rey," I answered.

"I like it," he said. I smiled. We listened for a while.

BRADY

It could've been five minutes, it could've been fifty, that we sat there in the dark, listening to her music, coming down from the greatest fucking blowjob of my life. The sweet girl was dirty as hell.

Daddy she'd called me. Theo had said she had daddy issues.

I turned to look at her. She felt my gaze and turned back to me, her expression open.

"Do you have some kind of daddy issues, Haven?"

She threw her head back and laughed.

"I'm serious."

Her laugh quieted to a smile. "Why are you asking that?"

"Theo might've mentioned…"

"Theo doesn't know shit," she snapped back.

"Alright?" I said, holding my hands up a little in surrender.

She smiled again. "I don't have 'daddy issues.' We've always been incredibly close. And, maybe… just maybe… being so far away from him, I'm attracted to older guys who make me feel… safe."

That made some sense. It was a little weird. "So, I remind you of your dad, huh?"

"I don't want to fuck my dad," she said, reaching over and touching my thigh.

This was an impossible thing. But we were already here. Again. And, I wanted to be inside her. Again. My dick was already getting hard again at the thought of it. I wanted to make her feel as good as she'd just made me feel. I wanted her to forget every guy that had ever been inside her. Starting with Theo.

I started to move my seat back up. It brought Haven's attention back to me. "What now?" she asked, seeming a little disappointed. I grabbed her jaw and brought her lips to mine, delving deep into her mouth, wrestling with her tongue and leaving us both breathless. She smiled. "Not home then?" she asked, a bright smile on her face and a mischievous look in her eyes.

"Get into the back," I said, stepping out of the car. She eagerly scrambled to follow out her own door. I opened the back door an she did the same. She started to take off her skates. "Leave them on," I demanded.

She smiled and climbed into the back, closing the door behind her.

"You have some kind of foot fetish, Brady?"

"Maybe. What's yours?" I asked as I lay her down in the back seat, spreading her legs to rest between them and rolled a condom onto my hardened length. She seemed surprised to see me ready to go so quick. "I guess I'm not that old."

"I told you," she said, reaching out for me.

"Wait a second, I wanna know your kink," he said, playing with himself, looking at my glistening sex. I brought my hands back and covered my face. "Are you embarrassed?"

"You already know," she said. That she liked to show up at my house in nothing but lingerie and a coat? That she liked it a little rough? It could be anything. I wanted her to say it.

"Tell me," I insisted, and ran a hand along her wet slit. She writhed a little. "Tell me."

"Look where we are," she said, breathily.

"In the middle of nowhere," I said.

"On a public road. Anyone could walk by," she said. "Anyone could catch us."

I laughed a little. "Public places?"

She nodded. "Is that bad?" she asked. I rubbed her again and she ground into my hand, gasping.

"It's hot. It's really hot. Maybe a little too dangerous in my position." It made me a little paranoid. But the turn on overcame it.

"I have never been caught. If it's any consolation," she added quickly.

"A little," I answered. I grabbed her thighs and dragged her a little toward me. "Now, where were we?"

"Please," Haven pleaded, pulling at my waist, almost panting at my tracing.

"What were the words you used?" I asked. She shook her head, a little desperately, senses leaving her as I ran my cock up and down, soaking myself in her juices. "You wanted to forget every cock before mine. Was that it?"

Her eyes flashed. "Yes."

"Yes?"

"Please." She grabbed at my shirt. I let her pull it off me. Her eyes trailed over my chest, my abs down the trail of dark hair leading to the cock that strained towards her. "Brady, please!"

I gripped her hips and pushed into her, feeling her hot tight wet cunt swallow my cock whole. She cried out as I stretched her out. I took a beat to look around. No one ever came up this road. There was nothing at the end of it. I pulled out again, lifting her legs a little and slamming back into her. She shot up a little, her stomach clenching as she cried out and fell back down as I pulled out again before slamming into her. "Yes," she started to say. Over and over, panting like a mad thing as I thrust into her. I pushed her legs further back toward her, making more room for myself and then worked to push her dress up. Finally, she ripped it off, freeing her arms to hold onto whatever she could, the head rest, the seat in front of her. Her nipples were hard and straining in her thin pink bra, as they bounced with every thrust.

I felt the sweat start to run down my back. I was blazing heat. I leaned over and bit her nipple through the lace, ripping a cry from her. She grabbed my neck and brought my lips back to her, sweeping her tongue in to taste mine before letting me go.

I fucked her hard, harder when I could tell she wanted it. Then harder again when she begged for it, until she was screaming my name and I was losing my vision with the pleasure of it.

"Holy fucking shit," she said, as I pulled out and sat back, shifting her legs onto my lap. Her head was lolling over, she was straining for breath, and the car was fogged over, like I had imagined it would when I dropped her at her apartment.

Twenty-two, I told myself as I discarded the condom and righted my clothes. Haven followed my lead and we found ourselves back in the front seat. Haven leaned over and sucked on my ear before whispering, "You're incredible."

"You're incredible, Haven," I said, turning back to her. She waited for me to say something else. To tell her we could do this again. But this was the second time I'd made this mistake and it couldn't become a third. I was already hating myself before I met her. I couldn't keep this up. I had warned her of dangerous habits. I wasn't going to let her become mine.

"Brady?" she said in question, looking at me hopefully. I started backing up the drive. Finally, I heard a click of the seatbelt and I knew we didn't need to have the conversation again.

HAVEN

Brady was a man, not a boy. He thought with more than his dick. That's where I'd gone wrong. He'd just fucked the living daylights out of me, and I couldn't bear to hear him say it would never happen again. So, I stayed quiet.

BRADY

Haven got out of the car, her feet bare, her skates in hand. I rolled down the window and she leaned in a little.

"I don't get this," she said. "What's the worst that could happen?"

I had thought up a seriously long list of consequences. But what was the worst?

"I could lose my kids," I said, trying and failing to do so lightly.

"Oh," she said, seeming to finally get it.

"I'm sorry," I said.

"Please, god, don't be," she smiled.

She nodded and said a silent goodbye before walking back into her apartment.

Never again. She seemed to believe me. I don't think I did at all.

HAVEN

On Halloween, I had an early morning shoot. And since I never could get to sleep before 11pm, I had barely four hours of sleep in total. That's why, when Odessa burst through my door at 3pm in the afternoon, I was wrapped up in my blanket, enjoying a nap.

"What are you doing?!" She said, throwing off my blanket.

"What does it look like?" I asked through my wake-up haze, grabbing for my blanket back.

"You need to get up," she demanded, keeping it from me. "We have a party to go to."

"What party?" I asked. Had she mentioned a party?

I opened my eyes to find her holding up two plastic wrapped costumes in either hand. One was a sexy bunny rabbit, the other a sexy Alice costume.

"I don't care where we are going, I am not going as a bunny rabbit."

"It's the white rabbit," she said. "And, this is my costume. You'll be my Alice."

"Oh," I said, confused. "Where are we supposed to be going?" I reluctantly sat up and rubbed my tired eyes.

"I have been invited to Hedda Klim's Halloween Party."

"What?" I asked in disbelief. "By whom?"

"You'll never guess!" She said, disbelieving it herself. "Etienne Charpentier."

"Oh my god," I said.

"I know. He called me, apologizing about the role. He said he wanted me, but the director wouldn't listen."

"That's sweet," I said. At least the incredibly talented Etienne Charpentier recognized my best friend's talent.

"He said she told him to invite whoever. So, you and I are going."

"Really? It's not... a date?"

"So, what if it is..." she shrugged. "It'll be a hell of a party."

I had heard of Hedda Klim's Halloween parties. Every year she was in all the magazines in her costumes. She always went all out. But... would Theo be there?

I asked Odessa the question and she shrugged dramatically. "Maybe. Does it matter?"

It really shouldn't, I told myself. There are probably hundreds of Halloween parties happening, I thought, and he could be at any of them. I could go to a party, I told myself. Maybe I'd meet a guy who rose to the Brady Witter level standards that I'd recently set for myself. Maybe I'd meet Brady. That was even less likely. I reached up and grabbed my outfit.

I wasn't sure why I'd been given the Alice costume and Odessa had taken the rabbit costume until we came out of our bedrooms within seconds of each other.

"Oh my god," I said, looking her up and down. Her rabbit costume was more burlesque than bunny. Extremely sexy. I looked frumpy beside her in my short puffy blue dress. I held the wig in my hands.

"You have to put on the wig..."

"It's itchy," I answered.

"At least for the first hour," she said, taking it from me and readying it. I tied up my hair and allowed her to put it on. The golden yellow blonde of the wig was really not my colour, but the lack of shoes with the costume meant that I could wear anything. I decided on a pair of combat boots to add a bit of punk flavour. That felt better.

"You look so cute," Odessa said.

"You look so sexy," I answered.

Odessa clapped happily. "Hopefully Eti feels the same."

"Eti?" I asked.

She just smiled bashfully. She liked him. That made me happy. She hadn't liked anyone for a long time. Her career had been more important. I hoped he liked her back. I hoped he didn't have some super annoying but annoyingly understandable reason for not being able to be with her.

BRADY

Cat had decided to let me take the kids trick or treating. Mostly because she didn't want to dress up and not dressing up meant being harassed on the street, ruining the occasion for the kids. I didn't mind dressing up. It just had to be dramatic enough to hide me well. I was told the kids wanted to be avengers and they'd determined I should be Thor.

I picked them up in the morning, only the girls again, and we spent the day playing with clay and catching up as best we could. At that age, it was hard to get much from Vera, but Zola told me all about school. I tried to find out about Mannix too, but the girls didn't have much to say about him. I told them to be sure and tell him how much I missed him. It felt cheap but I didn't have a lot of options.

I hired a company to bring the costumes in the afternoon. A few dressers came to the house and fitted the kids, Zola as Iron Man and Vera as Black Widow, and then me in a Thor costume including a pretty horrendous wig. One of our usual security guys who'd be going with us just in case, Leon, was fitted with a Hulk costume. He seemed to love it.

We spent a few hours trick or treating before the sun started to set and Cat wanted them home. We were stopped a few times but mostly the costume seemed to work as a disguise. Then we went home and changed out of our things. They emptied their little jack-o-lanterns into separate bags and then she came to get them. And, I was alone again.

After they'd gone, I looked over their costumes, laid out for collection the next day, wishing they could've stayed longer, wishing we could've done something else. Maybe visited a haunted house or had a Halloween party here with all their friends. The emptiness of the house was only emphasized after visitors. I'd been spoiled after so many years with a full and lively house. I had to get out.

I went for a ride down to Malibu and watched the last of the sunset. As I was preparing to get back on, I got a call.

Theo. Ugh. I answered.

"I have another offer for you."

"An offer?"

"There's a Halloween party tonight," he said.

"Oh..." I started, trying to think of an excuse.

"There'll be tons of people. Drinks. Food. Girls."

Girls... Maybe that wasn't such a bad idea, it might help me stop thinking about Haven. I shook my head at myself. I'd fucked Haven to get over Cat. Now I had to fuck someone else to get over Haven? It would be worth it if it worked.

"Okay," I said.

"It's a costume party," Theo said. "I'll text the address."

"Thanks."

He hung up then. I didn't have a costume. Other than the shitty Thor costume sitting in my living room. It wasn't exactly what I'd choose for an adult's Halloween Party. But those kinds of things left you the odd one out if you didn't dress up. It's kind of funny, I thought.

I rode home and changed back into the costume, refitting the wig and having a smoke in my backyard until a reasonable hour. I got a text from Theo at 10pm, saying he was heading over. I got into my Tesla and made the journey myself.

The street was packed with expensive cars. Mine was one of at least 20 Teslas parked on the lawn of a huge house. I didn't recognize it. I did recognize the people walking in. Aiden Hampstead. Joe Reagan and his wife Seraphina Valetta. It must've been a celeb's party.

"Brady!" A voice called out. I turned to find Theo in his usual casual get up. He slammed a hand on my back. "Great costume."

"Where's yours?" I asked, feeling like an idiot for dressing up.

Theo held a hand out to one of his entourage who handed over a plastic scary gorilla mask. He put it on. "How's it look?" He asked, his voice muffled.

"Swell," I said, sarcastically.

"Let's get fucked up," he said, leading me into the house. I let out my breath in a huff and followed. This was a terrible idea.

CHAPTER SIX:
Alice in Asgard

HAVEN

We arrived at the party, Alice in Wonderland and her White Rabbit, and immediately I felt underdressed. I was wearing a proper costume from a proper costume shop, but the rest of Hedda Klim's guests looked dressed by a film costume department; their hair professionally done, makeup too, even props in hand.

"We're way underdressed," I whispered into my White Rabbit's ear.

"I feel like a prostitute," Odessa said, suddenly self-conscious about the amount of skin she was displaying.

"You look great," I assured her, and then directed her attention to a group of women dancing on what was once a swimming pool but had been covered by plastic to create a dance floor. "They have way more skin on display." The girls were dressed as hula dancers, with coconut half shells covering their tops and grass skirts barely covering their G-string swimsuit bottoms. Odessa smiled at me, that seemed to make her happy.

"Can you see Eti?" She asked, searching the crowd.

I looked around and couldn't see his famous face in a sea of famous faces. "Oh my god, it's Missy Phegan."

"Where?!"

"There." I directed her gaze to where former model and now TV personality, Missy and her musician husband sat on a lounge beside other musicians and actors. "I love her."

"Let's go get a drink," Odessa said. We were standing around like fishes out of water. She pulled me back inside the incredible house to where a bar had been set up and we ordered ourselves some vodka sodas.

"Manning Nathan is standing behind you," I said, noticing the very tall, very muscular man behind her.

"Zane Ericson is sitting on the lounge over there, surrounded by Instagram models," She answered.

We laughed. What had our lives become? LA had a strange way of making this kind of thing seem normal.

We drank our drinks and kept moving through the house looking for Eti. When we had no luck, she took out a phone and sent him a text. "He says to wait here. He'll come find us."

"Okay," I said, finishing my drink and setting it down.

"Haven..." Odessa's voice was ominous.

"What?" She directed my attention to a group of men who had just arrived at the party and were being greeted by the surrounding people. Theo, his usual entourage and… Brady. Dressed as Thor? He wore a wig that looked like a stringy mop. But he looked good. He always looked good. And I looked more like a child than ever. Fuck. "We need to swap outfits."

"What?" Odessa scoffed.

"He can't see me like this."

"Theo?" she asked, confused.

"No, Brady. He already thinks I'm too young for him. I look 12 in this."

"It didn't seem to stop him from sleeping with you," she teased. "Twice!"

"He won't let it happen again because of our age difference. He doesn't want to seem like a creepy old man."

"That's refreshing."

"I'm serious, Odessa, you need to swap with me."

"Ok. Ok."

I looked around for the nearest bathroom, finding a small line leading towards one. I grabbed Odessa and pulled her with me.

"Odessa!" A voice distracted her and suddenly she was running into the long skinny arms of Etienne Charpentier. "You look.... Wow."

"You look pretty good yourself," she said, looking over his Ferris Bueller costume.

"Hey," he said turning his attention to me. "You must be Haven."

He reached out to kiss me on the cheek. "So nice to meet you."

"You too," he said with a kind of genuineness that was disarming.

"We actually were just running to swap costumes."

"Oh, why?" He said, quickly looking over Odessa's legs like he didn't want to have to stop.

"I think her reasons are null and void now," Odessa answered.

I turned to see what she meant but we were quickly descended upon by Carter and Damon Rousey. I'd recognized them as Disney child stars grown up, alongside Damon's girlfriend, Bella Karvan. She was a model I'd worked with before, but not closely, and long before anyone knew who I was. I doubted she'd remember me.

"Odessa, Haven, this is Carter, Damon, and Bella," Eti introduced us. Carter was dressed as Ace Ventura. Damon and Bella had come as some kind of anime characters.

"Hi," Odessa said, excitedly, as Eti put an arm around her.

Carter directed his attention to me. "I know you."

"Do you?" I asked, unable to keep from flirting with the handsome boy. With his dark hair, slicked back in a James Dean quiff, he was very cute. But I also thought he had a girlfriend.

"Haven Roser," he said, knowingly.

"You do," I smiled.

"He's a photographer," Bella explained. "We've worked together before. I am also a big fan."

I shook her hand. "As am I of you," I answered, glad to be proven wrong.

"I'd love to photograph you," Carter said.

"Say that a little creepier, Carter," Damon teased. Bella hit his chest.

"I'm down," I agreed. I had seen some of his work on Instagram and it was interesting.

"Can I get you a drink?" He asked with a nice smile.

"Don't you have a girlfriend?" Odessa asked, her protective instincts flaring.

"No," Carter answered, easily, returning his questioning gaze to me.

"Sure," I agreed.

BRADY

We stood out front talking to Belinda Carr and her husband, an app designer, for a good ten minutes before walking inside. I was already over it. But then I was struck by a painful sight. Haven was there, dressed like some kind of milkmaid meets rocker chick with a long blonde wig. She was talking to some kid. I could tell he was her age and dressed like Ace Ventura. He looked cool. I felt like an even bigger idiot.

"Let's go get a drink," I said to Theo, hoping to keep his attention from her. I failed nearly immediately.

"Is that Haven?"

Theo's friend, Cash, looked over confirming what I already knew.

"In a blonde wig. She knows I can't say no to a blonde. Maybe she did it for me," Theo joked, nudging me.

I paid him no attention. I watched as the kid she was talking to flitted away and then sighed, silently relieved.

"There is some serious ass here," Cash said, eyeing the beautiful women in the room. Hedda Klim arrived and greeted us quickly. She seemed shocked to see me. I apologized for just showing up without an invite.

"Are you kidding me?" She asked. "You're Brady Witter."

She quickly left us, attending to other guests.

"I'm gonna go say hi," Theo said, returning our attention to Haven.

"Why, man?" His friend asked. "There are plenty of good-looking women in here. There's a dozen in this room."

"You haven't fucked her," he answered. My fists clenched.

"True," his friend answered. But I have and I did not want him anywhere near her.

"Why don't we see what's happening outside?" I suggested.

"You go ahead. I'll catch up. Hopefully with Haven on my arm."

The Ace Ventura kid came back, drinks in hand, handing one over to Haven and suddenly she noticed me. Me and Theo both. Her cheeks flushed as she drank her drink and spoke to the boy, trying to pretend we weren't there, both of us staring at her.

"Look," I said. "She's busy with that kid. He looks about her age."

"Yeah. She's not into that. She's got daddy issues," Theo said, preparing to approach.

That fucking kid started playing with her hair like a creep. Shut the fuck up, Brady. This is exactly what she should be doing, not sucking you off in the front of your Tesla in the Hollywood Hills.

Theo left, with no warning, and walked over to her. Fuck.

HAVEN

Carter was playing with my hair, asking if I wanted to dance when I noticed Theo coming over. My heart was still beating wildly from when I saw he and Brady arrive. Why was Brady with him? He knew what an asshole he'd been. And, why did Brady have to look so good? Even in a dodgy Thor costume. The thought of our moments together made me bite my lip. Carter thought I was flirting with him.

"I'm down for a dance," Odessa said, looking to Eti.

"Yeah, let's," he said, leading Odessa out. Bella pulled Damon, too. I didn't move, too curious to see what Theo had to say.

"What about it?" Carter asked. He suddenly realized what I was looking at and let out an annoyed huff.

"Haven," Theo said, a warm smile on his face, his arms opening up as if he expected me to hug him. That was laughable. He held a hand out to Carter instead. "Theo," he said.

"I know. Carter," Carter answered, shaking his hand.

Theo turned his attention back to me. "You look great," he said, looking over my costume and taking a vape out of his pocket.

"I'm gonna go find the others," Carter said, resigned. He gave up easily.

I smiled, somewhat apologetically. Theo paid him no mind. His eyes were firmly clapped on me. "What do you want?" I asked, flatly.

"You look really good," he said, blowing smoke into my face and up my ass.

"Not fat?" I asked.

"I never said you were fat."

"Do you want me to go? This is an industry party, isn't it? I'll go," I feigned.

Theo laughed a little. "Okay. I'm a piece of shit. You made your point."

"You are," I agreed, drinking the vodka soda Carter had brought me.

"So, who was that kid? You dating him now?"

I shook my head.

"Good," Theo said. "You wanna come say hi to the boys?" He thought I liked his friends, but I never had. They were the more obvious, exaggerated versions of Theo himself.

"No," I answered.

"You wanna find somewhere to sit and talk?"

"No."

"How about we just go home then?" Theo reached over and touched my waist, pulling me a little toward him.

BRADY

I was two seconds from walking over there and kissing her, in front of Theo, in front of everyone, just stamp down the problem in a second. Well, maybe not the problem but a symptom of it. He pawed her like a doll. Why was she smiling at him? Surely, she wasn't so forgiving. He'd treated her horribly. Just go over there, Brady!

I took my first step, but her girlfriend beat me to it. Haven was suddenly being dragged out of the room. Good.

Theo started back to us. His friends teased him for striking out. "Game's not over, boys," he answered.

"Let's go outside," he suggested, taking vape juice from his pocket.

"I'll meet you out there," I said, leaving the group and searching for Haven. She stood in an empty corridor by herself, playing self-consciously with the lace at the bottom of her skirt. God, she was so beautiful, even covered up with all that shit. I could see her beneath it. There was a reason that Theo couldn't stay away, even with his policy of only dating stick figures.

She looked up and smiled. "Again," she said. "We have to stop meeting like this."

"Where'd your friend go?" I asked.

"Bathroom," Haven answered.

"She needed you for that?"

"She wanted to tell me not to go home with Theo," Haven answered. My chest tightened. "I like the costume."

I leaned against the wall alongside her. "I like yours."

"I don't suit the blonde," she said, tugging on the wig.

"Why are you talking to Theo?" I asked.

"Why are you here with Theo?" She shot back, turning to look at me head on.

"He invited me. I needed to get out of the house. Your turn. Why are

70

you talking to him?" It wasn't a good reason. He'd been an asshole to her, I shouldn't have been anywhere with him. But she shouldn't be talking to him.

"Is it making you jealous?"

"Violently," I answered, honestly.

"Really?" She asked, seemingly pleased.

"Don't go home with him," I demanded.

"Why not?" She asked, torturing me. "*You* won't go home with me."

I took out my phone. "Give me your number."

Her face lit up. "Really?"

I handed over my phone and she quickly typed her digits in.

"When are you leaving?"

"Does now work?" She asked.

"You don't want to stay?"

She shook her head wickedly. "Not if the other option is you."

"Go home when you're ready to go. I'll call you."

"Tonight?" She asked, as I bounded off the wall.

"Yes," I said. I walked away, feeling the smile radiating off her behind me. My willpower was in shreds. I wanted her. And, she wanted me. There was no reason we couldn't be together. I hadn't really done the casual sex thing for almost two decades. But I wasn't dead yet. Cat didn't have to know. No one had to know. I didn't have to tell anyone. I'd make sure she kept it quiet, too. She had so far. If I was going to give in, then I was going to give in all the way. I was going to allow myself to enjoy every part of her. And, I was going to have some fun.

First things first, a fantasy I'd been having ever since she told me her kink. No, before that. Since learning that she lived in the apartment building across from my favorite hotel. I went straight to my car and made a call. I booked a room, demanding the fourth level, street side, not my usual penthouse suite. I drove to the hotel and checked myself in. Then I waited.

CHAPTER SEVEN: The Voyeur and the Exhibitionist

HAVEN

Brady left and I stood there dumbstruck. He'd given in. Odessa came out soon after that and I told her I had to go.

"You said you weren't giving in to his charms!" She bemoaned.

"Whose?"

"Theo's?"

I shook my head. "I am not going with Theo. I can't tell you what it is, but I have to go home."

"Are you okay?" She asked, looking for some discernible sign of illness or pain.

"I'm really okay," I said. It was the wrong thing to say because her expression scrunched into something decidedly annoyed.

"You cannot keep bailing on me."

"What are you talking about? You're on a date!"

"Still... he's here with friends. I am supposed to be here with friends."

"Odessa..." I whined.

"Just another hour?" She pleaded.

"I can't..."

Her expression was desperate enough that I gave in. "Fine." But I didn't promise an hour. She took me back to a table set up by the pool/dance floor where the Rouseys, Bella and Eti sat waiting, drinking, and laughing at something we'd missed.

Carter's eyebrows shot up as I took the seat beside him. "How do you know Theo?" He asked.

"I don't really," I said honestly.

"He didn't win you over?"

"Definitely not," I answered, not meaning to flatter him at the same time. He did seem flattered. He and Damon shared a look.

"So how about that dance?"

I looked over to the cramped dance floor, the young couples grinding on each other. I did not want that to be me. I wanted to be back in that bar with Brady, grinding in the rain. "I'm not really a dancer."

"Aiden is here, Odessa. I want to introduce you." Eti lifted Odessa from her seat and took her away to meet one of his co-stars. She looked back at me apologetic.

"What are you then?" Carter asked.

I shrugged. "To be honest, I'm not feeling all that well."

"Oh no."

"Yeah, I might bail," I said. Odessa was perfectly fine on her own. I wasn't giving up another night with Brady.

"Really?" Carter asked concerned. I nodded. "Well let me drive you."

"Haven't you been drinking?" I asked.

"Not enough for it to be a problem," he answered. Before I could turn him down, he was saying goodbye to his brother and his brother's girlfriend.

"It's really okay," I said as he led me out of the party and toward his car, a sleek black Range Rover. He was insistent.

He held the door open for me and I got in.

He kept up the conversation throughout the drive. I tried to be polite but also make it somewhat clear that I wasn't interested. It struck me as I said goodbye, giving him a thank you kiss on the cheek and getting out of the car, that I wasn't more interested. He was definitely attractive. I could have easily flirted with him, danced with him, even gone home with him. But since meeting Brady, I had no interest in anyone else. He was in my system.

I rushed inside, rode the elevator to my floor and stepped into my apartment. Within seconds of stepping into the main living area, my mobile was ringing. A private number.

"Hello?" I answered, nervous, excited.

"He drove you home," Brady's voice was quiet, there was no noise in his background, he couldn't have been outside.

"Where are you?" I asked. He'd wanted me to come home. He must've been there somewhere.

"Theo. Carter. Who else do I have to worry about?" His voice was low, husky, jealous. I loved the sound of it.

I walked over to the windows looking out on the street below. "No one if you want me to yourself."

"I do." His answer came quickly.

I smiled. That was just what I wanted to hear. "Then I'm yours."

"Take off your dress," he said, commandingly. I was immediately turned on.

"Where are you?" I asked.

"Take. Off. Your. Dress." He punctuated each word. I stepped further into my living room, avoiding the light of the street lamps. I put my phone on loudspeaker and set it down on the floor.

"Come to the window."

Oh my god, I thought. He's on the street somewhere... or... I looked across the road at the building in front of me. The hotel he had mentioned he liked to stay at. He was in there. He was watching me.

"Flash a light," I said.

"You figured it out, did you?" He asked.

"Are you a voyeur, Brady?"

He shot back quickly. "Are you an exhibitionist, Haven?"

"I'll do my best," I said, approaching the window. "Flash a light. I want to see my audience."

A quick flash directed my gaze to the level above me. He turned it right off. He didn't want to be seen. But I knew where he was. And, I kept my eyes on his window.

I started with the wig, pulling it off, pulling out the bobby pins holding my hair up. I let it tumble down.

"Shake it out," Brady demanded. Good to know he liked that. I did as he asked.

"How's that?" I asked. He gave no answer.

"The dress," he prompted.

I reached behind me and unzipped the dress, dragging it down my shoulders, moving just a little, no music to dance to. It wasn't that kind of show. I pushed it down my torso and dropped it on the floor. I heard Brady's breathing pick up. I wore black lingerie beneath the dress, silk and lace, with black ribbon decorating it. I put my hands on the window looking up at him.

"What now, lover?" I asked. He laughed a little.

"Show me your body," he demanded.

I nodded up at him in response. I turned around, like he had turned me in front of him, the first time he'd seen me like this. I touched my body as he did then, feeling the curvature of my ass, the weight of my breasts, the softness of the skin on my belly, the length of my neck.

"Lay down," he said, clipped and breathy. The thought of his eyes on me was giving me all the confidence I needed.

I lay myself down on the floor, stretching out, my arms above my head, gyrating a little on the carpet. I turned over, onto my stomach, bending my knees, posing like I would for a lingerie shoot. I got onto my hands and knees stretched myself out like a cat.

"You're divine," he said, quietly. "I love to watch you."

"I like you watching," I answered.

I got onto my knees, and moved over to the window, my hands on the glass, looking desperately up at him. "I like it even more when you touch me."

"How?" He asked.

I took one hand from the glass, bringing it to my cheek. I tried to mimic the way he'd stroked my cheek when he'd kissed me. I used two fingers to touch the places on my neck where I remembered the sucking, the nipping, then my chest. I used both hands to knead my breasts, thumbing my nipples as he had. I felt his gaze; it was almost like my hands were his. My head fell back with the thought, the pleasure of it. I kept my hands traveling down my stomach, to where I wanted his touch the most.

I cupped my sex, already wet, just the sound of his voice had started that. I rubbed myself, using the lace of my panties for friction against my aching pussy, the lust overwhelming, shivers running up my spine.

"Brady... Come here. Or I'll come there," I said, rubbing heartily.

"You want me to take over?" He asked.

"Yes," I said, shifting my panties aside to touch my skin, feeling the slickness. "I'm aching for you."

"Okay," he said, pleased. But... "I want to hear you beg."

"What?" I threw an arm back up against the glass as I bent forward, my fingers delving into me. His fingers, I told myself. His cock.

"Beg," he said again.

I groaned. Was he serious? "You fucking sadist. Okay. Please. I beg you. Come and fuck me. Please, Brady. Please come fuck me." Whatever he wanted to hear, I said. If he was a sadist, then I was a masochist, because I was loving the sweet torture, this desperate longing, this teasing.

"Stop," he said then.

"What?" I cried out.

"Get your fingers out of your cunt." I reluctantly pulling my hand from my underwear. I fell back on the ground, petulant. "What's your apartment number?"

I smiled.

BRADY

I was running. I started running the second she said please. I kept the phone to my ear, listening as she moaned, pleading, desperate. I was at her elevator, but I needed her floor.

"302," she said.

I hit the button and was quickly going up. "Open the door for me," I said. "Then get back on your hands and knees."

"It's open," she said, quickly after. I arrived on her floor, running until I found her room. It wasn't far. I opened the door and walked inside, crossing the living room quickly. There she was, on her hands and knees. Her bra and panties still on, black as night. Her black biker boots on, too. They might've been sexier than the trench coat and heels.

She looked back at me from her position.

"Is this where you want to fuck me?" She asked. "Anyone could see."

My cock twitched. "Let them look. Let them wish they were the ones buried in you." Her head fell forward, as if the words themselves were giving her pleasure. I'd changed already, into jeans and a t-shirt. I started to strip. She watched me from her hands and knees, eyes roaming, taking me in, hungry.

"Turn over," I said.

She did as I asked, laying down on her back. I dropped my jeans, the last to go. I wasn't wearing anything underneath. She eyed my dick, bit her lip, fingers going to her cunt. I grabbed my cock, stroking it. I was hard the moment she dropped that blue dress on the floor. "I told you not to touch yourself," I said.

Her hands fell flat beside her. "You're touching yourself," she said, angrily.

"Take the rest off," I said. She worked to rid herself of her bra and panties, kicking away her boots as well. She lay stretched out, her chest rising and falling as she watched me stroke myself. "Please," she said quietly, impatiently.

I got down onto one knee and ran a hand up her leg, feeling her mound, the wetness there, before trailing up her stomach, following the pattern she'd made, up to her neck, her cheek. I ran my fingers over her lips. She licked out at them, writhing a little, her legs crossing as she squeezed tight. "I love how soft you are," I said.

I ran my hand back down, giving her what she wanted. "Yes," she said, as I started running my fingers up and down her slit, soaking them in her, circling her clit, before plunging into her warm, tight cunt. She grabbed onto my arm as she rode my hand, eagerly. She reached out for my cock, taking it in her hands working me as I worked her.

"Brady," She said, bringing my attention from her writhing body to her sweet lips.

"I want you in my mouth," she said. Those fucking words would destroy me.

"Your sweet lips say such dirty things," I said.

"I bet my sweet lips look even sweeter around your cock," she said then.

"Fuck," I said, and swiftly turned her around on the carpet, bringing my mouth between her legs, feeling her take my dick in her mouth, stroking me as she licked and sucked until she could only focus on her own pleasure. I had her screaming in minutes, gripping my thighs, her own legs shaking.

I moved off her, turning around to watch her writhing as she rode it out, keeping my fingers on her, rubbing, soothing, waiting for her to be ready to take my cock.

She opened her eyes to me lying beside her. "You're fucking brilliant," she said, turning to face me and bringing a leg over mine, opening herself up to me again. She kissed me, deeply, gratefully, before reaching to take me back in her hands.

"Hold on," I said, reaching out for my jeans, making quick work of the condom in my pocket.

She pulled me into her then, and I let us roll over, my weight on her,

her breasts pressed against my chest, her hair splayed out beneath her making her look like some kind of painting. I thrust into her over and over, as our movements, our breathing synced. She turned us over then, climbing on top of me, riding me, her hands holding my chest. She liked to be on top.

We lay there fucking, under the moon, the street lights, the possible other voyeurs in the building, but we were in our own world. I came hard above her and she came again quickly after, her walls clenching around me, screaming out in ecstasy. I loved how loud she was. Even in a building where her neighbors were likely to hear. She had no shame. I had none either. I loved to watch her come down from it. Her blissed out expression, flushed skin, fluttering heart.

I couldn't make out her face from my room in the hotel, and I didn't imagine anyone was lucky enough to have a telephoto lens at just the right time to capture us. But the thought was exciting. Even without that element, sleeping with Haven was exciting. The way we fit together, the way we could already talk to each other, the way she seemed to know what I wanted, and I knew the same of her. As much as I knew, I wanted to know more. I wanted to know everything.

* * *

The door banged open, waking us both up.

"Oh my god," her friend said, shielding her eyes with a bunny rabbit costume. I grabbed the blanket I'd brought out from Haven's room and covered us both, bringing Haven close to me.

"Odessa?" Haven asked drowsily.

"I am so sorry. I will be in my room."

Keeping her laughing face covered, she rushed through the living area and into the other bedroom, slamming that door as well.

Haven looked up at me, awake then. I thought she'd smile, say good morning. She looked a little sad. "What's wrong?" I asked quietly, wrapping my arms around her.

"So, are you gonna tell me that's it? The last time."

"What do you think?" I asked.

"I think you're willing and able to torture us both." It would seem that way from the last few days. But...

"I'm not. I've long lost the will. I want this."

"What?" she asked, surprised.

"I want this," I repeated.

"Oh my god," she said, reaching up to grab my neck and bring my lips to hers.

"For now," I said, when she finally let go.

Her eyebrows furrowed. "What does that mean?"

"It means," I started. "We spend time together. Get to know each other. Casually. No strings."

"You want me to date other people?" No, I said, in my head. I'd fucking hate that. But I couldn't give her everything she needed.

"Yes, if someone your age, who can give you the things that I can't—"

"Like what?" she demanded.

"Like the ability to walk down a street without being harassed."

"You know that's not always possible for me either," she answered, reminding me of the night I found her skating.

"You know what I mean." She nodded. "We can spend time together until someone right for you comes along," I said.

"Okay," she said, hiding a smile.

"But it needs to stay between us. Can you do that?"

There was her smile, wide and pleased. "I can keep a secret."

CHAPTER EIGHT:
A hazy shade of bliss...

HAVEN

He wanted to spend time with me. He wanted to get to know me. It had never been purely sexual for me, but three out of four of our encounters had ended the same way. We hadn't had a conversation that lasted more than a few minutes. I'd worried that he was only interested in the one thing. Which honestly would've been okay considering how mind blowing the sex was. But I wanted more. I thought maybe he'd been keeping me at a distance, making it easier to keep sending me away. But no more.

After Odessa asked to come out and eat breakfast, we'd hurried into my bedroom and got into my bed. Brady said he hadn't slept much, the floor being less comfortable for him than his body was for me. He curled me into his chest and fell asleep in minutes.

I couldn't sleep any more, but I wanted to stay in his arms. As I was slowly turning in his arms, positioning myself to watch him breathe like a weirdo, my phone started buzzing. Shit, shit, shit, I chanted to myself as I reached to my bedside table, trying to shut it off before it woke Brady.

A groan alerted me to his waking, and I shifted just enough to grab it just as it stopped. I turned back to see Brady rubbing his face and opening his eyes. "Good morning," I said, apologetically.

"Is it still morning?" he asked.

I lit up my phone and gave the time. "Almost midday."

My phone started ringing again. "Mom."

I silenced it. "Go ahead," he suggested.

"I can talk to her later."

"Can I use your shower?" he asked as he got out of bed and pulled on his jeans.

"Of course," I answered. "There's fresh towels on the rack."

He smiled at me and walked out the door. I answered the phone.

"My girl, where have you been?" My mom sounded exasperated.

"Sleeping," I answered. It was sort of true.

"At this time of day. Tell me you're not partying at all hours of the night," she groaned.

"I'm not—"

"Cause that's not why you're there," she insisted.

"I know," I agreed, not that she had any right to tell me what I could and couldn't do anymore. "How's Dad?"

"He's good," she answered.

"Is he there?"

"Um, no," she paused. "I'm not sure where he is."

"Okay well tell him I said hi," I offered, ready to hang up on her.

"I will. Wait, I have to tell you about Joan. She's been cutting out pictures of you to give me."

"What?" Joan was our elderly neighbor back in Anchorage.

"She's so proud of you."

"That's great," I said, cringing a little at the idea of old biddy Joan seeing me in all my lingerie ads.

"I think she prefers you over her own grandchildren. That youngest boy is causing all kinds of problems in that family…"

I took a breath as my mom started gossiping about Joan's youngest grandson, who I used to smoke cigarettes with secretly behind her tool shed. He'd been caught dealing weed a few months ago and now apparently had knocked up his elder brother's girlfriend. It was hard to blame my mother for gossiping when the gossip was so juicy.

Brady came back into the room, still in his jeans but his hair and torso dripping and godlike. "Mom, I have to go," I interrupted her.

"Oh, okay. Call me tomorrow?" she asked.

"I'll call you soon," I answered before hanging up. Brady dried his hair a little more with the pale blue towel in his hand and sat on the bed. "How was your shower?" I asked.

"It was okay," he answered. "You could use a better shower head."

I laughed a little. "What's wrong with it?"

"It's just weak."

"You like a strong manly shower, do you?" I teased.

He tossed the towel at me, laughing.

"My turn?" I asked.

"You should shower at mine. Are you doing anything today?" he asked.

I tried to contain the massive smile threatening to spread. "No," I answered.

"Come over," he suggested.

"Okay," I agreed. "Now?"

"When you're ready," he answered.

I jumped up and rushed to the door. "Gimme a few minutes."

I rushed into the bathroom and quickly washed my face before starting to brush my teeth.

"What are you watching?" Brady's voice said.

I ducked my head out to see Brady leaning on the couch where Odessa had arrived and started up Netflix.

"*Gilmore Girls*," she answered.

"Quality show," Brady offered.

"Good taste," Odessa replied, pleased. I smiled through my toothpaste.

Brady turned to see me watching, I ducked back inside, speeding up the brushing until I saw him arrive at the bathroom door. I hurriedly spit and washed my mouth.

"Hi," I said as I popped back up.

"You should pack a few things," Brady said.

"Really? Already?"

"If you want. Makes things easier if you end up wanting to stay over."

"Okay," I said. He smiled and walked away. Things were definitely different now. I heard my bedroom door close and started back across the living room. Odessa and I clapped eyes as I walked, silently screaming at each other before I walked back into my bedroom.

Brady stood at my shelves looking at my photos. "Are these your parents?" he asked, holding the picture of them from their twenty-year anniversary.

"They are," I answered.

"You look like your mom," he offered.

I took it as a compliment. "Thank you."

"What's she like?"

"She's pretty good as far as mothers go. She's the slightest bit overbearing. I think she struggles having me so far away."

"Do you go back often?"

"Rarely," I answered regretfully. I took some clothes from the drawers and started changing.

"Hold up," Brady said. He jumped onto the bed, throwing his arms behind his head.

"Comfy?" I asked.

"Ready," he answered.

I started changing, trying to look sexy but failing. "It's sexier taking things off."

"I hate to tell you, you're sexy either way."

I picked up my skinny jeans, regretting the choice but unwilling to put them back. "This is gonna be less sexy for sure."

I started bringing them up, struggling over my thighs before falling back onto the bed and sucking in to pull them up. I looked back to find Brady smiling. "Still sexy," he answered. "Come here."

I crawled up the bed toward him, kissing his lips gently.

"Good morning," he said.

"Morning," I answered, before shuffling back off and picking up a bag to pack a few more things.

"Are they still together?" Brady asked, looking back to the picture of my parents.

"They are. They've been dispassionately married for twenty-five years."

"Why do you say that?" he questioned.

"Cause when you tell people they've been together for twenty-five years the response is all awe and admiration and it doesn't feel deserved in their case," I answered.

"You don't think they love each other?"

"I don't know," I shrugged. "I think they stay together out of habit."

"Have they ever been passionate? Maybe they're just not very passionate people," he offered.

"My mum is an extremely passionate ice skater—"

"Which is how you got into it," he guessed.

I nodded. "And, my dad is strangely obsessed with fly fishing."

"Really?"

I zipped up the bag and shuffled my feet into a pair of black mules. "Ready?" I asked.

He jumped up, throwing his shirt on and shoving his feet into his shoes. I led him out of the room.

"See you later," I said, as we passed Odessa.

"Bye. Bye, Brady," she said, turning to watch us.

"Good to meet you," Brady offered.

We took the elevator downstairs and we paused at the doors. I guessed his train of thought.

"Did you want to bring your car up? I'll wait here," I suggested.

"Okay," Brady agreed. "Let me take this." He grabbed the bag from my hands, touching my hands softly as he did, before walking through the doors and out onto the street. I waited a few minutes before the black Tesla, its dark windows betraying nothing, pulled up in front of me. I ran out and jumped in.

BRADY

Haven was good at the under the radar thing. Her time with Theo must've trained her well. I hate that I was doing the same thing to her.

She jumped in, buckled up, and we were off. I couldn't help but recall what we'd done in that same car only days before. I saw her smile in my peripheral vision. I guessed she was thinking of the same. I put a hand on her thigh, and she covered it with hers.

"Are you hungry?" I asked.

"I could eat," she answered. "I could really do with a coffee."

We stopped a nearby café and Haven ran in to get us two coffees. Mine black, hers with ice.

"How come ice coffee?" I asked her.

"It's just how my mom always made it," she answered. "I'm sorry about your mom."

So, she knew then. "Thanks," I said, returning my hand to her thigh.

"Do you see your father often?" she asked.

"Not for years," I admitted.

"How come?" she asked. "I don't mean to pry."

"No, it's fine," I assured her. "We never got on well. Especially after my mother passed."

"I'm sorry," she said again, squeezing my hand on her lap.

I brought the conversation back to her. "Do you have any siblings?"

"No, it's just me." Both only children, I thought. Cat had a very strange relationship with her brother that was at times very cold and at others a little too intimate.

We pulled into my driveway and into my garage where the passenger side door opened up beside my bikes.

"Do you think you have enough bikes?" she joked, looking over the three that sat there.

"Yeah, I have a few," I answered.

Something in my expression must have given me away. "This isn't all of them, is it?"

"These are the ones I ride regularly."

She gasped a little. "How many do you have?"

"It's hard to say," I answered.

"What do you mean?"

"Have you heard of Lucciola Motors?" She slowly shook her head. "It's my brand."

"You make bikes, too?"

"I'm partnered with a guy who designs and builds custom bikes."

She smiles, shaking her head a little. "What does Lucciola mean?"

"Firefly. In Italian."

"I like that," she said. She touched the black leather seat of my Harley.

"Have you ever ridden?" I asked.

"No," she answered.

"I'll take you," I offered.

"Really?"

"You want to go?"

"Definitely," she said, enthusiastically.

"After breakfast," I said, taking her hand and bringing her inside.

I took her into the kitchen and pulled out a stool at the breakfast bar for her before taking out all the ingredients for a hot breakfast.

"You're going to cook for me?"

"I'm going to give it a red hot go," I answered. "My kids don't really enjoy my cooking, but I'm trying."

"That's sweet," she tilted her head a little.

"What do you like?" I asked.

"Everything. Anything," she answered but it turned out to be a bit of an exaggeration. She liked bacon but she didn't like steak for breakfast. "Too heavy."

I cooked her up a feast of bacon and eggs, followed by a few fluffy banana pancakes.

"You're a great cook, I don't know what you're talking about," she assured me.

"These are new skills. I had a chef come in and teach me a few things," I explained.

"Wow. Rich people," she scoffed. "At least you cook. Theo ordered in almost every meal."

I twitched a little at the name.

"Sorry," she said quickly. "I shouldn't be comparing you two."

"You're good," I assured her.

I started soaking a few dishes in soapy water and packing the dishwasher. She jumped up and took over, pushing me out of the kitchen. "What are you doing?"

"The chef doesn't clean," she said.

"Let me help," I argued.

"No," she said, turning back to the dishes. I got in beside her and kept going. She wrestled the dishes from my hands, and they landed with a splash in the sink, soaking her. She gasped.

"Oh shit," I said, laughing as a clump of suds fell from her nose onto the floor. She looked back at me with a wicked glint in her eyes. "Don't—
"

She grabbed a handful of suds and threw them at me.

"Really?" I asked, as they dripped down my chin. She just smiled. I rushed at her, reaching for the sink through the arms she threw up to block me. I started tickling her to bring her hands down and she bent forward, cackling. "Give up?"

"Never!" she proclaimed through fits of giggles. I kept at it, tickling her until she was in a ball of hysterics on the floor. "Okay, I give up!"

I pulled her up by the waist and she leaned into me, her back against my chest.

"You play rough," she said, her breathing slowing.

"I thought that's how you liked it," I whispered into her ear.

Suddenly two palms full of suds were thrown into my face and Haven was running out of the kitchen. I chased her through the house, dripping suds everywhere, nearly slipping on the marble floors as she flew down the hallways and finally into my room. She backed into a corner, her hands raised apologetically, as she pleaded to be spared. I walked over to her as menacingly as I could. "I'm sorry, I'm sorry," she said, smilingly. I stood in front of her, looking down at her. "What are you gonna do?" she asked.

Quickly, I dropped down, picking her up and throwing her over my shoulder. She squealed a little at the surprise and held on tight as I ran with her into the bathroom.

"Oh my god, don't!" she said, as I turned on the shower and got in there with her, soaking her in the cold water. "It's freezing!" she screamed.

She reached for the taps to turn the hot water on, but I grabbed her hands and held them against the wall. "Do you give up?" I asked again.

"Yes," she screamed.

"You swear?" I asked, leaning closer to her, pressing my forehead against hers. She took a breath, pressing her chest, again mine. I felt her nipples hard beneath her shirt.

"I swear," she said, breathily, her amusement turning to want.

I let go of her and turned around to turn the water to warm. I felt her approach behind me, taking my arms in her hands and pressing a kiss to my back.

The water began to run warmer as she lifted my shirt up and over my head. I turned around and looked at her, watching as she ran her hands over my tattoos.

"What do they mean?" she asked, touching the tornado on my waist and the script over my heart.

I looked to the tornado. "This is the way my life changed, how I could've spun out of control and still could if I don't take care."

She bent down and kissed and licked at the ink there. I took her hands and brought her back up. She kissed the script on my chest and then read; "However vast the darkness, we must supply our own light."

She looked up at me for an explanation. "It's a Stanley Kubrick quote. About finding meaning—"

"In life," she finished. "I get it."

Something about that stopped her. I made a note to ask her about that later. She touched the dates etched into my shoulder. "The kids' birthdays."

She nodded. I tugged at her own shirt and lifted it up and over her. I took in her wet chest, her nipples straining towards me in her bra. I touched them gently, bending a little to take one of them into my mouth. Haven's hands went to my shoulders, feeling the light line ridges of the tattoo on the left side of my upper back. "This one?"

"Howl's Moving Castle," I explained. "Zola's favorite book."

We went on like that, undressing, kissing, touching, explaining my tattoos while worshipping her unmarked skin until there were no more clothes to be shed and no more stories to be told. I grabbed a condom from the drawer and she took me into her mouth before rolling it onto my cock.

I lifted her up into my arms, pressed her against the warm tile walls and plunged into her hot core. She moaned, reaching up to hold on to the window sill above the shower as I hammered into her, feeling the water on my back and all the sensations building at once. I watched her tits bounce as she rode my cock like a wild thing, panting desperately. I leaned forward, taking her nipple into my mouth and biting down. She cried out and let go of the sill, grabbing onto my neck and holding me close.

I pulled out of her and dropped her onto her feet, turning her around in one swift movement and pushing back in. "Fuck!" Haven groaned, falling a little forward, using the tile wall as leverage to meet my every thrust.

I ran my hands over her soft round ass cheeks, running my thumbs over the thin silvery lines there before running my hands up her back, to her shoulder to bring her back up to me. She came up, moaning, turning her head and sticking out her tongue to touch mine. I grabbed her breast in my hand and brought the other down to her pulsing soaking bundle of nerves, her hands covered mine, nails digging in as I played with her, teasing as I fucked her hard until she was begging me to let her come. I opened my mouth on her shoulder and bit down just as I squeezed her clit. She threw her head back screaming as her walls clenched around me. I held her up, thrusting along with the waves of her orgasm until my cock jerked deep inside her.

HAVEN

"I'll never get sick of that," I said, coming out of the bathroom in one of his fluffy white towels. He'd changed into leather pants and a white shirt. "Or that," I said, looking him over.

"You still wanna go riding?"

"Isn't that what we just did," I joked. He smiled. "I didn't bring any leather pants."

"Jeans are fine," he answered. "I have a jacket for you somewhere."

He went off, I guessed in search of it and I changed into jeans, combat boots, and a matching white t-shirt. He came back with a men's black leather motorbike jacket that I coveted immediately. "Hope this is okay," he said, helping me on with it.

"Okay? It's gorgeous. I feel like Debbie Harry," I said, referencing my mother's favorite rocker chick from the 80s.

"You know Debbie Harry?" he asked.

"I know plenty of old school music," I answered.

He laughed.

"Go on, test me," I teased. "Eurythmics, Billie Holiday, The Everly Brothers—"

"I believe you," he said, taking my hand and pulling me from the room.

"But do you know Billie Eilish?" I asked.

"Sure," he answered as we walked through his house to the garage.

"Harry Styles?" I asked.

"The kid from the boy band."

"What about KPop? Ever heard of BlackPink?"

"BlackPink in your area? I have daughters," he answered. "No wait, that's weird."

I laughed. "We'd get on great!"

"I'm sure," he answered, handing me a white full-face helmet before putting on his red open-face helmet. He climbed onto the low riding Harley and then gestured for me to climb on. I did so, without much grace and he clicked a button to bring up the garage door while starting up the bike.

The engine roared. He turned back a little. "You alright?"

"Fine," I answered.

"Hold on," he called. I wrapped my arms around him, feeling his tensed abdominals and he took off slowly, out of the garage and down the driveway. Another click had the gate opening up in front of us and he checked with me again. "You ready?"

"Yeah…" I said, my voice slightly shaky.

"You'll be fine," he promised and took off with none of the previous trepidation.

"Oh my god!" I screamed, as the wind whipped by us. The engine rumbled beneath us, the noise like something out of hell. But all too quickly, I was accustomed and even enjoying the sound. The other cars flew past in a blur as we navigated around them, speeding down the Hollywood Hills streets.

We finally stopped at a set of lights. He touched my hands where they gripped him tightly.

"Are you o—"

I cut him off. "This is amazing."

I heard him laugh a little as the light turned green and we took off again. He took a turn and suddenly we were on the highway, going faster and faster, like nothing could stop us. I loosened my grip on him to lean back a little, feeling the wind travel up my neck, through my loose hair. "I love this," I said to myself, over and over. "I love this."

He settled into the straight path ahead and put a hand on my knee. Feeling brave and stable enough, I touched his hand where it sat, squeezing it tightly. He seemed to take a hint and put his hand back on the bars, taking us faster and faster. I gripped his stomach as he wove in and out of lanes, speeding ahead of everyone. I felt wild, maniacal, free. I wanted to scream. So, I did just that, throwing my head back and screaming. I felt his stomach muscles expand and retract as he laughed, obviously hearing me. We kept going until we were on the highway to Malibu, the winding turns bringing our bodies close to the road on each side. If I reached out, I could've touched it. I imagined my hands going through the blurry concrete like a wave.

Then he was taking us up through the Malibu Hills, until we stopped on a corner overlooking the ocean. He climbed off ahead of me. He removed his helmet and set it on the bars before helping me with mine. I was breathless. He helped me off the bike and my legs felt like jelly, from the position or the adrenaline, I didn't know. "How'd you like it?" he asked, a bright smile on his face.

"I fucking loved it," I answered, jumping into his arms and kissing him.

"I'm glad," he said.

I looked around for a beat. "Are we okay here?" I asked.

"We're good," he assured me. He seemed to know all the private spots. Most of his life as a famous movie star was probably the cause of that.

I walked over to the guard rails and looked out over the water. The sun was setting. "This is beautiful," I said.

He came to stand beside me. "It is."

"Thank you for bringing me here," I said, bumping into him a little.

He wrapped his arms around me. "You're welcome." We held each other like that, swaying a little, as we watched the sun set, burnt orange, like the dress I wore the night he picked me up skating.

When the sun was finally down, I turned around, wrapped my arms around his neck and kissed him. I thought I tasted a little salt, maybe from the ocean air. He put his hands in my hair, kissing me back, nipping at my lips before pulling away to kiss up my neck. "You taste so good," he said, sending shivers from the top of my head to the tips of my toes.

"We should get off the road," I said, wanting to find somewhere a little more private.

"Yeah," he answered, running his hands down my back and squeezing my ass. "Let's go."

We walked back to the bike and I touched the handles as he put on his helmet. If it felt that good to ride it… I imagined what it would feel like to be in command of so powerful a thing.

Brady came up behind me. "You wanna learn to ride?"

I turned, surprised. He seemed serious. "Am I allowed?" Didn't you need some kind of licence?

"No one's around," he answered with a smile.

"Okay," I said, nodding enthusiastically.

"Climb on," he said. I did so, leaving my helmet where it was. He talked me through all the switches and mechanisms of the bike. "You got it?" he asked.

"I don't know," I said honestly, getting a little nervous.

He climbed on behind me as I put on my helmet. He kicked up the kickstand and then reached under my arm to turn the key.

"I'm going to be right here," he reassured me. "We'll go slow."

"Okay," I answered. "I'm ready."

"Let the clutch out a little," he said. I did as he said. The bike started moving forward, on its own weight. I was riding. Slowly to be sure, but riding. I cackled a little. Brady laughed behind me. "You wanna give it a little throttle?"

I turned the right handlebar just a little, but it was enough to stall us, and we jerked to a stop. Brady laughed a little behind me. "Don't laugh!" I mocked outrage.

"You gotta be gentle then shift into second." I lifted my hands as he showed me. He pulled in the clutch and clicked at the clutch pedal. "I'll do the pedal. You focus on the rest."

"Okay," I said, as we started up again. We shifted into gear fine but then I did something wrong and we stalled again. Brady laughed at me again. "Hey!"

"It's not easy," he assured me, apologetically.

"Do you want me to control it?" he asked.

"How?"

He set us up again and put his hands on the handlebars.

"Put your hands on mine," he suggested. I did as he said. And then we started moving. With my hands on his, mirroring his movements, it felt like I was commanding the bike. His body kept me still and steady, as he sped us up. We rode around those Malibu Hills streets, feeling all the power of the bike beneath us as the night turned cool and dark. When we returned to that same lookout, we swapped back around, and Brady took us home.

The day had been long and I was exhausted. I wanted to enjoy the fact that I'd be sleeping in Brady's bed, but my body was ready to pass out. I didn't want to close my eyes. Or if I did, I wanted to wake up to another day just like the last.

"This was a great day," he said, before I could.

"Thank you," I said.

BRADY

She caught me staring as she woke up. I smiled, perfectly content to be caught in the act.

"Hi," she said. I moved toward her, taking her lips in mine and shifting back. I rolled over onto my back and brought her with me. She nestled into my side and ran her small hand over my chest. She fingers seemed to linger on the script over my heart.

"You got a funny look on your face when I told you about this tattoo."

"Did I?" she asked.

"How come?"

"I don't know. I guess it reminds me of things my mother used to say. She was always on me to find a passion."

"Ice skating?" I asked.

"First that."

"Was she bothered when you stopped?"

"No. She was never trying to live her dreams through me or anything. She always just wanted me to be happy. She wanted me to find that thing I loved. Like ice skating for her. And, fly fishing for my dad."

I felt stupid saying it. "Modeling isn't a great passion of yours?"

She laughed a little. "No. Not that it can't be challenging."

"Not everyone has to find some great passion in their lives. There's something to be said about enjoying the little things."

She nodded. "Yeah. I don't know."

"You're still so young, too."

"Am I? I didn't realize," she teased.

She touched the skin beneath my right eye. "How come you have this ring around your eye?" she asked.

"It's heterochromia. I've had it since I was born." The ring of brown was thin and ran around my pupil before the blue of my eyes took over.

"It's pretty," she said.

"You're pretty," I answered, pressing a kiss to her lips.

"You're one to talk," she teased.

"Do you have anything like that?" I asked. "Birthmarks? Scars? I know you have no tattoos."

"Do you know that?"

I lifted the covers, looking at her bare body, searching for any mark of ink as she laughed and kicked softly at me.

"You won't find it," she said. I came back up.

"Where is it?" I asked. She lifted up her arm, showing me the inside of her wrist. I couldn't see anything. "Where?"

She looked brought it back to her face and pressed a finger to a spot, slightly off center. I brought it back to me and looked closer. She was right. The smallest of peach colored hearts were there.

I smiled. "It's cute."

"Thank you," she said reluctantly. "You probably think it's kind of wussy compared to yours."

"Not at all. I have three kids. I'm in awe of what pain the female body can handle."

She laughed a little.

"What's it mean to you?" I asked her.

"My mom always said I wore my heart on my sleeve. From when I was little. I always liked the idea of it."

Just as she'd done to mine, I brought her wrist to my lips and pressed a kiss there. Her mom was right. Everything I knew of Haven from the past few days had shown me she was open to the world. She never seemed to pass judgment on anyone without cause, was trusting of everyone, and had shown me so much of herself unfearingly. She was wonderful. It made me worry. But I watched as she noticed the creases above my brow, the tension displayed on my face. I watched her lifting two fingers to smooth them away, running them from my brow to my temple kneading them away. I let the worry go too.

HAVEN

At first, I counted the days. It all felt like a dream. I liked him so much. He was so funny, so intelligent, so effortlessly cool and beautiful. I was counting firsts, too. The first time he held my hand. The first time he sang to me, trying to make me remember a song I'd never heard before. The first time he rubbed my feet after a long day of shooting in the highest of heels. The first time I could see myself growing old with somebody. I had to stop counting. I wanted to be in the moment. Especially if it wasn't going to last.

I couldn't stop thinking about him. On the days he was with his kids, or the days we both had work. I had a few trips coming up and I dreaded being so far away. I liked to just be in his company, even if it meant holing up at his place. We had it all to ourselves. Until the doorbell rang one afternoon.

"Are you expecting someone?" I asked, as he rose up from the couch to check the security camera.

"Holy shit," he exclaimed. "It's my cousin."

I jumped up. "Should I go?"

He considered for a moment before speaking. "No. Stay."

"Are you sure?" I asked. "I don't mind," I assured him.

"No, you're good. You're fine," he answered, before buzzing his cousin up.

I walked over to him, feeling slightly nervous.

"Should I say…" I wasn't sure if I would be pretending to be something other than the girl he was seeing. Was I about to pretend to be the cleaner or something?

"Yeah. She can know," he assured me.

I was surprised. I had just assumed the cousin would be a man. A beautiful young dark haired woman came driving up to the house in a red Porsche. She got out of the car with flourish and rushed over to the door where Brady and I stood waiting.

"Billy boy!" she said. Another surprise. I knew his real first name was William, but I'd never heard anyone call him by that, especially not a nickname version of it.

"Sabine, what are you doing here?" he asked, hugging her tightly. She looked at me over his shoulder, curious.

"I'm visiting a boy I met online, don't judge me," she pulled away and turned her gaze back to me.

"Oh, I definitely won't be doing that. Sabine, this is Haven," he introduced me.

She held out a hand and smiled brightly, genuinely. "A pleasure to meet you, Haven."

"And you, Sabine."

"Come in, come in," Brady said, ushering us inside.

I stepped aside and Sabine stumbled a little over the shoes I had left there haphazardly. I felt suddenly ashamed of having made myself too at home. "Sorry about that," I said, shifting them out of the way.

"No worries," she brushed it off and looked around. "So, this is the new place? It's a bit…"

"Plain?" Brady asked. "Cold? I know."

"I was going to say—"

I took a guess. "Sterile?"

"That's it! Like a hospital," she laughed.

Brady looked at me a little pitifully. "Is it that bad?"

"No," I said gently at the same time as Sabine said, "Yes."

"You need a decorator," she continued. "In a major way."

"Yeah, I'll get on that," Brady answered. "So how long are you staying?"

"Just the night. Hopefully," she teased.

"Please don't tell me you're planning on staying with some stranger you met on the internet?"

"I said don't judge me."

"Tons of people are meeting online these days. It's not just the weirdos anymore."

"That sounds like a Broadway song," Sabine declared before singsongingly, "it's not just the weirdos anymore!"

"I didn't mean you," I said, suddenly flushing. Open mouth, insert foot.

"No, I know what you're saying," Sabine continued. "But it's hard out there for a single gal of my age."

"Surely not for you. You're beautiful," I said. She really was. She had a similar color of ice blue eyes as Brady but long dark hair, a slim build, and an incredible amount of energy I could already tell.

"You're a sweetheart," she said. "She's a sweetheart," she turned to Brady.

"She is," he agreed.

"You two are…"

Brady swallowed before answering. "Dating."

"That's great," Sabine spoke without hesitation. "I feel like I've seen you before."

"She's a model," Brady answered.

"That must be it. And, how old are you, Haven?"

"Sabine..." Brady seemed to warn her.

I looked to Brady, but he was eyeing his cousin. He had told me she could know. "Twenty-two."

Sabine pursed her lips and let out a breath of air. "I see."

I straightened up, not interested in being put down if that's where this was headed.

"Where are you from Haven?"

"Alaska," I answered.

"Alaska," she repeated. "You came here looking for fame and fortune? You found the right person to attach yourself to."

"I didn't attach myself to anyone," I defended. Who the hell was this person?

"I get it. He's my cousin but even I want to bang him sometimes."

"Great, I'll leave so you two can get it on," I quipped back.

Brady looked at me, eyebrows high as a slow smirk spread across his face.

Sabine suddenly cracked up. "That was good."

"There's something wrong with you," Brady said as he went to the fridge and grabbed a beer

Sabine made her way over to me. "Really, best comeback yet." I let myself laugh along with her.

She threw an arm over my shoulder and brought me into the kitchen.

Brady handed us a couple of beers.

"I was just joking. We only bang our second cousins back home."

"And, where's that? Hell?"

Sabine cracked up again and Brady laughed, too.

The laughter broke all the tension. Sabine seemed to like to test people. But after the test she was all sweetness and hilarity. Brady ordered a few pizzas and we all relaxed into each other's company for the night, eating, talking, laughing, and drinking. Brady drank more than both of us combined, in the best of spirits to see her. It meant he headed to bed early, as Sabine and I ate the ice cream in his fridge for dessert.

"So, how'd you meet Brady?" she asked, when he was out of earshot.

"At a party," I answered. "Restaurant opening thing."

"Fun. How long has this been going on?" I was worried about another test, but she seemed genuinely curious.

"A few weeks, I guess."

"Wow."

"What?" I asked.

"I'm just shocked it's not longer. You two are so easy with each other."

I looked back at the hallway where Brady had gone. "It is easy," I shrugged.

"Wow. But you are young," she continued.

"Yeah. We're not really telling people."

"I see," she nodded. "Catalina would flip."

"Right." I shoved the ice cream away, done. "Well, she's never going to find out so…"

"Never?" Sabine asked, taking the ice cream for herself. "Are you done with this?"

"It's all yours."

"What do you mean never?"

"We're just hanging out for a little while. It's casual. Impermanent."

"Impermanent?"

"He's just waiting for me to meet someone my own age. Apparently."

Sabine laughed. "Chicken shit."

"What me?" I asked.

She coughed a little on the ice cream. "No, him." She changed her mind. "Maybe both of you."

I took a breath and sat back in my chair, looking up at the stars.

"Anyway, I'm glad he met you. He's been pretty down the last few months," she said, bringing my attention back to her.

"He has?"

"After the separation."

"Of course." The way she said it though, so seriously, made me curious. She scooted her chair back and stood up.

"I'm going to get some sleep."

"Okay. Good night."

"Good night," she said, passing me by and heading to the guest room where we'd put her bags.

I cleaned up the table outside and the mess in the kitchen before heading back to Brady's room. He was sleeping soundly, so I hopped in the shower for a few quick minutes before climbing into bed with him.

He woke immediately with the movement and automatically wrapped me up against his chest.

"Hey," I said quietly, nestling into his warmth.

"What were you two talking about out there?" he asked.

"Nothing," I said, a hint of a stutter.

He pulled back a little, reaching down to pull my chin up to look him in the eyes.

"She wasn't giving you shit, was she?"

"No," I assured him. "But…she said that you'd been down lately."

He nodded. "I guess so. Post-separation blues," he admitted.

"It sounded a little more serious than that," I tested, wary of making him admit something he wasn't willing to. "Was it… were you depressed?"

I waited quietly, feeling the pads of his fingers trace patterns in the small of my back. "Maybe a little," he admitted.

"Why? Why do you think it was so bad?" I asked, hoping he was willing to open up.

"I guess I felt like a failure. I failed at marriage. I failed my kids."

"You didn't fail them," I said, too quickly. Let him speak, I told myself.

"I abandoned them. And, the home we shared."

"You didn't. Why do say that?" I saw him on the phone to them, almost every day. He saw them once a week or more. I knew it wasn't much, but he certainly hadn't abandoned them.

"Not like I should be. I should be there every day. Cooking their dinners. Tucking them in." His voice was breaking a little. It hurt to hear. I ran a hand through his hair, smoothing back the loose curls.

"I'm sorry. I'm sorry it's so hard. But it's not your fault. These things just happen."

He nodded. I took hold of his chin and brought his lips down to mine, bring his lower lip between mine and sucking gently. Brady brought his hands under me, pulling me up and onto him as he rolled onto his back. I straddled him there, kissing him deeper, feeling his legs clamp hard on my thighs, feeling his growing hard-on press between my legs.

"Really?" He had drunk quite a bit.

"I don't know if anything could stop me getting hard with you nearby."

"Your cousin is really close," I reminded him.

"Then we should be really quiet."

"I don't know if I can do that," I laughed a little. He laughed with me.

"I'll just have to cover your mouth then," he said, rolling us over again.

Brady started undoing the buttons of my pajama top as I pulled down his boxers with my feet.

"That's a clever trick," he said, kicking them off his ankles and ravishing my chest with his lips and tongue.

"I have a better trick than that," I offered, taking him in my hands.

He groaned at the touch as I ran my hands up and down the length of him, pumping him a little before squeezing his balls in my hand eliciting another groan.

"You have to be quiet too," I reminded him.

"I'm not the problem here," he said, pulling my pajama shorts down and away, feeling the slickness already gathered there.

"You're soaked," he whispered.

I reached into his bedside drawer where I knew I could find condoms and handed one over for him to put on while I rid myself of my pajama top.

He got himself lined up. We were both too impatient to delay. He pressed the head into me, and I let out the softest of cries before he clamped a hand over my mouth. I tried to speak, to beg for more, he was too still. I shifted my hips up to take him in deeper, moaning in delight, as his forehead fell into my shoulder and his hand clamped down harder.

We tried to keep ourselves quiet, but eventually it seemed pointless. And I wanted to hear every delicious sound he made. And, he seemed to enjoy mine. He fucked me into oblivion, and I screamed the house down.

BRADY

In the morning, we found Sabine in the kitchen. She gave no hint that she heard a thing and Haven seemed relieved. She was taking photos out of a box I'd left in the spare room wardrobe. There were pictures of my mother that I hadn't seen in a long time. We sat down and looked. Haven sat on the floor, by my legs, looking at the pictures I gave her.

Sabine had to go and meet her date but made me promise to put up some photos around the house. I assured her I would. Haven said her goodbyes and I walked Sabine out.

"Good luck with your date," I offered.

"Good luck with yours," she said, a pitying look in her eyes. I wanted to ask her what it was about, but she was already driving away.

I walked back inside to see Haven still going through the pictures.

"She's beautiful," she said, holding another photo of my mother.

"She was," I agreed.

"How old were you?" she asked. "When it happened?"

"Twelve," I answered.

Her eyes scrunched up. "That must've been unbearable."

I nodded. "It was." That was the right word for it.

"Especially to bear alone, if your dad wasn't very present." I worried I'd told her too much. She was so easy to talk to. And telling her the things I had, felt like a weight off my chest. Every time I opened up to her, I felt lighter.

She looked up at me. I nodded, unable to think of what to say. She looked back at the photos. "This might be overstepping… but I could buy some frames, put up a few of these. If you want me to."

"Really?"

"Sure. Easy peasy. I'll order online. Everything will come straight here…"

"Okay," I nodded. "I'll give you my credit card."

"Okay," she stood up. "Where's your laptop?"

I went to grab my laptop from the office and realized the room made up of a desk, chair and lamp, was just as 'sterile' as the rest of the place. I came back with my laptop. She popped it open and got started.

"You know if you wanted, you could get some other stuff," I suggested.

"You offering me a spending spree? Am I your Pretty Woman?"

I laughed. "I meant for the house."

"Oh," she laughed back. "Yeah. I'd love to. I've kinda been dying to."

"Well go for it," I said, taking my credit card from my wallet and handing it over.

"Thank you," she said, a wicked smile on her face.

"Don't go wild," I warned her. "But do feel free to get yourself something pretty if you like. As a gift for helping me out with all this."

"I can buy my own pretty things, Brady."

"I know you can," I squeezed the foot that lay by me on the couch.

She squeaked a little and brought it back to her. I turned on the TV to watch as I let her shop. Now and then she turned the laptop to show me what she was considering. She had unsurprisingly great taste.

✳ ✳ ✳

A couple weeks later and my house was feeling much more like a home. To take deliveries and just for ease, I'd given her a key to the house. Haven accepted the disclaimer like it was nothing. But I had to admit, I liked to come home and see her shoes by the door. Even if I was in a shitty mood from traffic in downtown LA, and a billboard image that I couldn't erase.

Haven was laying on the couch, her feet up on the arm rest.

"Hey!"

She sat up quickly, embarrassed to be caught relaxing like she was. I didn't think she had to be. I liked seeing her so relaxed in my home. I tried to rid myself of the day's tension with a beer.

"How'd your day go?"

HAVEN

"Fine. The shoot was long," I answered. "I'm glad to be off my feet." I hoped he didn't mind that I'd just lazed out like that on his lounge. I'd spent the afternoon after my shoot putting the finishing touches on the place and I was exhausted.

"Have you ever thought about doing anything else?"

I flinched a little at the line of questioning. "Yeah. All the time. These opportunities won't last forever. Looks fade. I'll have to figure out something else eventually."

"I don't think that's something you need to worry about for a while," he said.

"Why do you ask?" I questioned him.

"There's a billboard of you downtown, did you know? It's massive. And, you're naked."

"I'm not naked," I answered. My friends had texted photos of the billboard since it went up. "It's called lingerie."

"You look beautiful," he said. "I'm jealous of all the people looking at you every day."

"You get to look at me every day," I reminded him, enjoying this direction a whole lot more.

"I'm okay with that," he answered. "It's the other motherfuckers I have a problem with."

I smiled. "I hate to say it, but I quite like this jealousy."

"You do?" he asked. "You don't think it's pathetic?"

"No," I answered. "I just thought you were encouraging me to find one of those motherfuckers."

He stiffened up. Shit. Wrong thing to say.

"I was just joking," I said quickly.

"No, you're right. How's that going?"

"What?"

"How are you doing finding somebody?" He seemed to have put up a wall very quickly.

110

"I didn't realize I had to be actively looking…"

"You don't."

"Is there some kind of use by date on this?" I asked, feeling myself getting angry. I told myself to pipe down. I didn't want to have this conversation. I didn't want him thinking any harder on the subject.

"There sort of is," he said.

"I'm going to go for a swim, is that okay?"

"Um…" he stilled.

I stood up and stripped down then and there, doing my best to end the conversation.

"It's fine," he said finally, as I walked out and dived into the pool.

I let the cold water soothe the dull thudding of my heart, a warning of pain soon to come. My head broke the surface as I rose back up and saw Brady standing at the edge of the pool, his shirt off, his hands undoing his pants.

I smiled. If I tried hard enough, I could pretend I had not a care in the world. "Coming in?" I asked.

He nodded. I paddled back a little giving him the room he needed to dive in. I ducked my head backward into the water back to slick my hair back. I was surprised by a hand clamped around my foot dragging me down to the depths. I took a rushed breath and let him bring me down, clawing up my body with his hands until I was firmly in his grasp. I pushed the hair away from my eyes as we stilled there, deep in the water. I let the air out of my mouth as I saw him move toward me. I put my hands on his neck and he put his hands on my cheeks and we met in the middle, kissing each other like something out of movie until we were too desperate for breath to stay under.

He kicked off the floor of the pool and brought me up with him. We broke the surface together, sucking in the air we needed before bounding together again. This kiss had something desperate in it. Our tongues fought wildly. Our teeth knocked together and we barely noticed.

He pushed us to the edge of the pool, to a step I didn't know was there, where I let myself rest as he pulled my underwear off and away. His hand cupped my sex, before dipping a finger into me, grinding the heel of his palm against my clit. I cried out. He gave me another finger and I threw my arm over my face, biting the skin on my hand to keep from screaming as he pumped his fingers in and out of me, furiously.

"Is this the jealousy?" I said, in quick spurts, barely able to form the sentence.

"Could be," Brady answered, his gaze on my body, watching as the water moves in waves over my undulating body.

"Feels like you're ma… mad at me," I said. It didn't feel bad.

"I'm not," he answered.

I cried out again as he gave me another finger.

I couldn't speak. I wanted his hand on my neck. I wanted him to choke me. I reached out for it, taking it from my hip and dragging it up my body.

"What do you want?" he asked. "Tell me what you want?"

"I…" I couldn't say a thing.

With each pump of each fingers, each agonizingly good stretch of my cunt, I was riding closer and closer to my orgasm. I wanted to choke as I came.

He rubbed his hand over my chest, over one breast then the next, flicking my hardened nipples before coming back to the center, rubbing me on the chest, just below my neck, just below where I wanted it.

"You gotta tell me what you want, Haven. I'm not a mind reader." Suddenly it clicked. He knew. He knew exactly. He was torturing me.

Angrily, I threw his hand away before falling back as another wave of pleasure shocked me with its force.

Suddenly, his hand slammed against my neck, forcing my head down against the edge of the pool, his grip strong and sure. "I know what you want. I know."

His hands moved faster, pumping in and out of my cunt as his grip on my neck got slowly tighter and tighter, the air becoming harder and harder to suck in through the small space he left for me.

I'm going to come, I thought. I brought my hands away from the edge of the pool, putting one on the arm he used to finger fuck me and the other on the wrist of the hand around my neck.

Brady played me like a fiddle until I was coughing as I came, choking for breath as the orgasm exploded at my core and sent electric spasms all over my body like violent ecstatic fireworks. Finally, his grip on my neck released and I sucked in gasps of air like a dying man.

I felt blind. I felt senseless. I was hot and wet and shivering. Slowly I came out of the pool. Brady was carrying me. He carried me through the house, bridal style as I continued to come down until he set me in his bed and I fell back to earth. He tried to pull away but I held him close. "Hold me?" I plead.

He got into the bed beside me, took me in his arms and held me gently, caressing every part of me until he reached my neck. He pressed a kiss there. "Are you okay?" he asked.

"Yes," I assured him. "That was… unbelievable."

"Are you sure?" he asked, his voice sounded small.

I kissed him deeply in answer before bringing my lips to his ear to whisper. "I'm not ashamed. I like what I like. And, I love it with you."

✳ ✳ ✳

Throughout the next few weeks, as he got into the first shooting block of his new film, we saw each other less. I traveled for fashion week and to shoots outside of LA, but he started calling me, just to talk. It became a sort of ritual when either of us was away, to call in the evening and talk about our days. I'd drink a glass of wine, getting drunk on the red and the sound of his voice. Sometimes those conversations would grow dirtier and dirtier until we were touching ourselves, helping each other get off in our respective locations. It was never as good as the real thing. How could it be?

When we were home, we started itching to leave the house. He started to take me riding on his bike. I'd wanted to go again since our first ride. He and his bike were recognizable, so we were sometimes tailed, photographed by paparazzi, but the helmet kept me and my identity hidden. We'd drive out to hiking trails and hike for hours. He loved to be active. I didn't so much but I liked it with him. I loved to hear him talk about his kids. I was glad to know he was such a good dad, even though things were rough as he was working through his divorce from Catalina.

It was becoming harder and harder to claim that what we were doing was just casually sleeping together. I liked him as a person, for more than that face or body or how good we were together. I liked spending time with him. I wanted to go out with him. To restaurants or movies or to see people. I wanted to talk about him, brag about him and how lucky I was. But I couldn't tell him that. Because the secrecy was his idea, he was protecting his reputation, and mine according to him. He couldn't get past the age difference, so I had to try and just enjoy what I had of him.

BRADY

Haven and I spent weeks in a kind of hazy bliss. She worked more and more and I had started shooting a new film but we found enough time. When we were together we'd talk, laugh, fuck, watch movies, and eat good meals. We spent a little time at her place, and I got to know her friend some, but mostly we stayed at mine. Sometimes we went out but only in ways that we could still hide. I took her riding. We went hiking. When either of us were too busy with work, or away for work, we'd talk on the phone. Fuck over the phone. I couldn't seem to go too long without seeing her or speaking to her. That would be a problem. Not one I wanted to acknowledge any time soon. I was too busy enjoying her. Her liveliness, her beauty, her kindness. The way she talked about her family, lovingly and unselfishly, was admirable. And, the way Odessa was with her, Haven was beloved back. Not to mention that it was the best sex I'd ever had. And, that was seriously saying something.

Cat had seen pictures of me and Haven out riding. She didn't know who the girl on the back of my bike was, and I refused to tell her. She didn't like that. I assured her that, if I ever became serious with another woman, then she'd know. She said I wasn't to introduce the kids to anyone without her written approval. Not that I had any plans to introduce Haven, ever. It couldn't happen. But she was still making things difficult.

On a long weekend off, wanting to spend some time out of the country, specifically in my Tuscan villa, but also not wanting to be without Haven, I flew her to Italy. She'd been of course, mostly to Milan on a biannual basis for fashion week, but she'd never been there for leisure. Knowing the hypocrisy of wanting to save our environment while flying private, I made the exception for this case. We couldn't be seeing traveling commercially together. Surprisingly, she'd never flown private before. It was fun seeing her enjoy the novelty of it. Then watching her as she took in the house, the vineyard, as we arrived at the Villa, she was awed by it. I was awed by her.

We took a tour of the winery and she tried some of my vintages. She loved red wine, I knew, but I was glad she liked my wine specifically. Even the driest of them, and I knew she wasn't a fan of dry, she said she liked. We had a barbecue out on the deck and watched the sunset over the vines. We made love in the spare bedroom. I didn't think she'd want to use the bed I'd shared with Cat. Maybe I didn't want to either.

The weekend was heavenly. Neither of us wanted it to end. We took one last walk among the vines. I fed her a ready grape but when I tried to kiss her, she teasingly ran away. I chased her through the rows, watching her long hair fly behind her, her dress billow, flashing the length of her legs. I caught her and we fell down onto a patch of soft grass at one end of the land and made love right there. Made love? I needed to stop calling it that.

We reluctantly flew home, but she had to fly out again straight away to Hawaii for a shoot. We didn't bother going to either of our places. We picked up my car, drove it a little way from the airport and took to the backseat to fuck one more time before another separation. I drove her back to drop off and kissed her goodbye. She seemed as sad to go as I felt.

I went home and unpacked and went to work the next day, already missing her. She sent me a few pictures from her shoot. They'd painted her body as if she wore a bikini. I hoped a woman did the painting. I spent the day checking my phone, which I usually made every effort to avoid, much to the chagrin of my director and cast mates. I tried to turn my phone off, but my finger just wouldn't hit that button.

A few nights later, my long-time friend, another actor, Gregory, came into town and came over for drinks and dinner. He'd seen the pictures, too and wanted to know who was on the back of my Harley. I tried to avoid the subject, steer him away from it, but he was insistent.

"You can't tell anyone," I said, deciding to give in to him. "I'm serious."

"Should I be worried? She's not married, is she?"

I shook my head.

"Underage?" He questioned next, jokingly.

I took a breath and Gregory's eyes widened. "Not underage," I said, quietly.

"So, she's young," he guessed. I nodded. "How young?"

I dropped my head, nervous for this one piece of information most of all.

"I'm not gonna judge you, buddy," he said.

I looked back up. "Twenty-two."

Gregory let out a breath in a whoosh. "Wow." He shook his head a little, he wasn't prepared for that number. Neither was I when it walked into my life.

"I haven't gone that young before," he said. "Not since I was that young."

I nodded.

"Even dating someone in their thirties has been tough for me the last few years. I'm glad I've found Malia." Gregory was nearing sixty.

She was a great woman. Intelligent, confident, beautiful, driven. She was in her mid-thirties when they met. "What's the age difference?" I asked, not able to remember.

"Sixteen years," he admitted. "What's yours?"

"I can't bring myself to say it."

He did the math himself. "Twenty-three years."

"God, I hate myself," I said, folding forward in shame.

"Don't," Gregory said, clapping a hand on my back. "It's not that much greater than mine. And, I've had the same number before, or more than it."

I remembered those girls.

"Do you like her?" He asked.

"Yeah," I said, immediately.

"Then fuck what everyone else thinks. You just ended things with Cat. You deserve to have some fun."

"What if it's not just fun?" I asked.

Gregory nodded. "Then you have to be okay with the bullshit. People are gonna say horrendous stuff. About both of you. You'll be hounded by the paps. Cat will hate it."

He was never a fan of Cat. He almost seemed pleased about how much she'd hate it.

"That's the biggest worry. What if she tries to keep me from the kids?" I asked.

"Do you really think she would?"

"I don't know. I don't know her anymore," I answered.

"If she tried, you'd fight back, and you'd win. It's plain to see the great father that you are." He clapped a hand on my shoulder.

"So, who is she?" He asked.

"Haven Roser," I said.

His eyebrows furrowed; he didn't know her.

"She's a model," I added.

"Shit," he said. "That's even worse. You got a picture?"

I took out my phone and found a few pictures, she'd sent me. Nothing private. He took the phone from me.

"Oh wow. She's... she's... I mean, I get it."

I laughed a little. "If you didn't have Malia... if this had happened to you. What would you do?"

"I don't know, man. I can't tell you that. It would depend what she meant to me. If I could see a future, her age wouldn't stop me. But I'd have to be sure."

I nodded, that made sense.

"But our situations are so different. I don't have kids for one. I'm not going through a divorce. I already have the creepy old guy dating young girls rep."

"I never wanted that for myself," I said.

"Neither did I," Gregory said.

We laughed a little.

"Well good luck to you," he said, raising his glass. "You're gonna need it."

We clinked and drank, and I spent the rest of the night in quiet contemplation. She was coming back to town the next day. I volunteered to pick her up from the airport. I'd even had the shooting schedule shifted a little to allow for it. I couldn't help but think about this path we were on and how it couldn't continue indefinitely. If we kept it up, we'd eventually be found out. There seemed to be two choices. The first, we could allow ourselves to be found out, date like normal human beings, become boyfriend and girlfriend. 'Hey, this is Haven, my 22-year-old girlfriend.' Possibly lose the respect of everyone I admire, possibly lose my fucking kids. Or... we could end things. No one would ever have to know. She'd go on to date guys her own age. Carter Rousey. Or some other twat. And, I'd date someone my own age. And then, hopefully, I'd forget about her.

She came out of the doors looking every bit as beautiful as when she'd walked through them. Her hair was down, looking longer than ever. Her skin was newly tanned. Her eyes were bright as she searched the cars for mine. She found it then and rushed toward me, a smile on her lips. I opened the door for her, and she got in, throwing her overnight bag into the back seat and crashing her lips to mine. Any thought about choices to be made pushed way down while I savored her taste, her smell, her body falling against mine.

"Hi," she said, breaking away from my lips and looking into my eyes. "I missed you."

"I missed you, too."

HAVEN

I ran straight to Odessa's bedroom, making sure she was gone, before running back to Brady, pushing him against the door that he'd closed behind him. He dropped my bags on the floor and lifted me up by the thighs, turning us around, pushing my back into the door, pushing his crotch against mine, kissing me deeply, then moving from my lips to my cheek, my jaw, my neck.

"Bed," I said, and he carried us there, throwing me down and hurriedly stripping as I did the same. He pulled off my boots, my jeans, my panties and then fell forward onto me.

"Fuck," he said, tearing his lips from mine. "I don't have a condom."

"I do," I said, reaching over to my own bedside drawer. I opened it up and searched for the small blue packet.

Brady shifted off me as I looked in the drawer. I had one. I knew I had one. Oh my god.

"Fucking Odessa," I said, annoyed. She'd been dating Eti. She told me they'd been fucking all over the apartment while I'd been away. All my bets were on her.

"Fuck," Brady said, falling onto his back.

"Well, there are other things we can do," I said, reaching out to take his cock in my hand. He smiled, letting himself relax into my touch. I rolled into him, kissing his chest, shifting down the bed as I kissed his abs, the little trail of hair leading down to his hardened cock. I took him into my mouth, taking his firm ass in my hands. I felt his own hands touch my head, take root in my hair. I licked and sucked, letting him fuck my mouth until his hands touched my cheek, stopping me.

"Wait..."

"What?" I asked, looking up at him.

"I really want to be inside you," he said.

I wanted that, too. My cunt was pulsing, desperate for him. I'd been craving him for days. Not his fingers or his tongue. "I'm clean," I said. I'd been tested months ago, and we'd never gone without a condom.

"Me, too," he said. I believed him.

"I'm on the pill," I added. I had been since I was fourteen, specifically for my skin.

"Is it okay?" He asked me.

I nodded insistently, crawling back up his body, lining us up. He ran his hands over my curves.

"I missed you so much. You're so fucking sexy."

"Thank you," I said feeling as good about myself as anyone had ever made me feel.

He felt my cunt, the wetness there, the heat. He lifted one of my legs, opening me up and rubbed himself along the length of me. He groaned.

"Is that better?" I asked.

"So much fucking better," he said, before kissing me again, his tongue probing as his dick did the same.

"I need you," I said, gripping his neck. His hands grabbed my ass and he pushed into me, filling me up. God, the fullness, the feel of him, it was hard to breathe.

We took our time, went slow, feeling this together, without the sheathe between us, for the first time. We couldn't go back after this. It felt too good. Too right. The rightness was as overwhelming as the mounting pleasure in the pit of my stomach. The heavy, pulsing, coiling ecstasy growing inside me, ready to explode. Three little seemingly harmless words formed on the tip of my tongue. What? Where the fuck did that come from? I pushed them down. I couldn't say it. He couldn't hear it. But there was no lying that in that moment, that is exactly how I felt. And, the way he was looking at me, the intensity in his blue eyes, I could've convinced myself he felt the same way.

CHAPTER NINE:
Birthday Girl

HAVEN

The next morning, I woke up alone. I heard some tinkering in the living room and wandered out in a fluffy robe to find him looking through my shelves, at my DVD collection.

"What do you think you're doing?" I asked. I suddenly realized that I had a lot of Brady Witter movies and he was looking directly at him. Would that freak him out? Would he suddenly think I was a crazy stalker fan?

"Who knew you were such a fan?" he said.

"I told you I liked your movies."

"You've got them all," he said.

"Not true. I don't have all those bank robbing movies. Or that Vietnam one." He laughed a little. "I'm just a movie fan. You happened to have made some good choices." I jumped onto the couch and looked over him in his white boxers, crouched down in front of my TV.

"What's your favorite?" He asked.

"Depends on my mood," I said, teasingly.

"What's your favorite of my performances?" he asked, a more objective question.

"You need your ego stroked, do you?"

He laughed a little. "If you're doing the stroking."

"*Meet Jim Brown* was the first I saw. *Fighters* was great. Then there is the classic, *Fiona and Luann.*"

He laughed a little, remembering. "I was so young."

"You were gorgeous. And, so good. Not just the stuff where you were flirting with Jenna Dean but the interrogation with Harry Christie. You were already so good. And, that accent..."

"You like that?" He asked, in that same southern twang.

"I do," I answered, giving him the same accent back.

"Oh, you're good," he said, surprised.

"Thank you. A southern accent ain't that hard."

"You got any others?" He asked.

"If I've recently watched something British then I can mimic it rather well," I said, in an Emily Blunt-esque accent.

He found *Fiona and Luann* in the collection and brought it out, looking at himself.

"I was so young," he repeated.

"Can I see?" He threw the DVD my way.

"You were so skinny," I said. The picture on the back of the case had him shirtless, with a cowboy hat on and a hair dryer in hand.

"You calling me fat?" He joked.

I threw it back at him. He looked at it again and then put it back. He came to join me on the lounge.

"Do you wish I looked like that?"

I moved over to him, wrapping my arms around him. I touched the wrinkles around his eyes. "No," I said, honestly. "I like these."

I ran my hands over the ink on his chest, his stomach. "And, these," I continued.

"You got a thing for old men?" Brady asked, less teasing and more careful.

"No," I said. "And, you're not old."

"Who was the oldest guy you dated before me?"

"Theo," I answered.

"Who else?"

I angled my head a little, unsure why we were having this conversation. But if he wanted to know... "I dated a stockbroker in New York. He was 36."

"That is still a lot older than you," he said.

"He was awful. We had four dates. The fourth was a pity date."

"Who else?" He asked.

"I dated a model before him. He was 27. We dated for about 9 months. He dumped me for another model," I explained.

"What about before him?"

"Just my high school boyfriend. Ryan. We broke up when I moved to New York."

"Does he still contact you?" He asked.

"He comments on my Instagram. Sometimes he'll DM me to see how I am."

"Do you think he still wants you?" Brady asked, pulling me by the thigh to straddle him. I put my hands on his shoulders.

"We never had sex," I answered.

"Really? Who was the first?"

"The model."

"Was he good?"

"Nothing like you," I answered, taking hold of his neck, leaning in to press a kiss there.

"What about the stockbroker?" He asked.

"We never—"

"Wait, so it is just me, the model and Theo?" He asked, counting my partners.

Is that what this was about? "Yes," I said, furrowing my brows at him, mildly embarrassed by my lack of experience. "I'm only 22."

"Was Theo good?" He asked.

"Why do you need to know?" I asked. "Why do you want to know?" I wouldn't have wanted to be tortured by these kinds of details. Maybe because I was confident that all the women he'd slept with before me were more experienced, more beautiful, in every way better than me. Brady didn't have the same confidence.

"You don't have to tell me," he said. "I'm just curious."

If he wanted to know then I wanted to tell him. "He was fine. Obviously experienced. But what are you really asking? Are you the best I ever had?"

He smiled. "Am I?"

I shook my head, laughing a little, embarrassed to admit. "I wanted to cry thinking I'd never sleep with you again. I've never been able to talk so clearly about what I want. Sometimes I don't even have to say it, you just know."

His eyes widened, his smile too.

My turn, I thought. "How many have you had?"

"You don't wanna know," he said.

"I already know about the public ones," I said. "Hard not to."

"Honestly? I don't really know. I had some wild years. In my teens and twenties."

"Where do I measure up?" I asked, shyly ducking my head. "I know I'm inexperienced. You don't have to worry about hurting my feelings."

He gripped my jaw, bringing my eyes up to look at him. "You wanted to cry?" He asked me. "I've never spent so much time obsessing over a woman before. At work. With my kids. You're all I've been thinking about."

I leaned in close and kissed him gently, wrapping my arms around him, melting into him.

"How many did you love?" I asked, quietly.

He stiffened a little. "You wanna know that, too?"

"You started this conversation," I shot back. He nodded, he knew he had.

"Two," he admitted. "Cat and Gwendolyn."

Gwendolyn was also an actress. A tall stunning blonde who'd won Oscars and married a Rockstar. And then Cat, another stunning actress meets activist. I couldn't have felt smaller.

"Can I ask what happened with Gwendolyn?" I asked.

"You don't know?" he asked, slightly bitter.

"I read…" he nodded for me to go on. "I read she left you a few days before the wedding."

He swallowed. It must've still been painful to him. "I went to work and came home to find a letter and the ring in an envelope on the kitchen counter."

"Oh my god, not even in person." Brady shifted away from me, letting me go. "What was her reason?" It was too personal a question, but I really wanted to know.

He laughed a little darkly. "She said she was too young to be married."

Oh my god, I thought. He stood up and walked into the kitchen. His first love left him practically at the alter because she was too young.

I turned around to look at him searching the fridge mindlessly. "How old was she?"

He didn't turn back. "25," he answered.

Holy shit. My mind started turning quickly. His mother died when he was twelve. His father emotionally abandoned him. His first love left him, saying she was too young to be married at 25, he second love seemed to change her mind about him quicker than changing her clothes. No wonder he's so fearful of abandoning his own children. No wonder he won't take me seriously. Despite everything about us together feeling so good and right. In his mind, I wasn't a real option. And, maybe I never would be.

✳ ✳ ✳

We ate cereal at my kitchen counter. It always amused me to see him sitting there. A grown man in a girly shared apartment, eating cereal from crappy bowls on a Target stool. But I could barely muster the energy to smile. Odessa arrived home from Eti's and found us that way, eating quietly.

"Hey, if it isn't my world traveler." She came over and gave me a strong hug. "Missed you."

"Missed you too," I said, as she gave Brady a hug. That was the first time they'd done that, I thought.

"How is the boy?" I asked, not sure if Odessa wanted Brady to know.

"He is good," she said, smiling. "I'm dating Etienne Charpentier. Have you—"

Brady cut her off. "I know him. He's brilliant."

Odessa smiled, agreeing. "He's been helping me plan your birthday," she said to me. "He thinks we should do dinner at this new Thai restaurant... What's it called... Something Alley."

I looked immediately to Brady. He shifted a little uncomfortably. "When's your birthday?" He asked.

"This weekend," I said. "Twenty-three," I said, knowing that sounded a little better than 22. Just barely.

He swallowed, suddenly nervous.

"Are you coming, Brady?" Odessa asked. My head flew to her, my brows furrowed. Of course not. She knew this. She didn't like that he wanted to keep us private, but she knew. I didn't begrudge him for not coming. I wasn't even going to tell him, to avoid any discomfort. I was going to tell him I was going out for a birthday, and just leave out the fact that it was my own.

"Haven's parents are flying in from Alaska," she said. Yet another reason that I knew he wouldn't want to come.

"Odessa," I said warningly, before turning back to Brady. "She knows you can't come. It's really fine."

I could see the warring in his head. He could feel the judgment coming from Odessa. I eyed Odessa venomously. She seemed to back down and left us to our breakfast.

"Brady? It's really okay."

"I'm working this weekend anyway," he said.

"There you go," I said, hoping to end the conversation.

"I better get ready for work," he said, getting up, emptying his bowl and putting it into the dishwasher. I nodded as he walked back into the bedroom. Bloody Odessa.

Brady went to work, with the briefest of kisses, and I ran into Odessa's room to chide her.

"I'm sorry," she said, though she didn't seem to mean it.

"Don't you like him?" I asked.

"Of course," she said. "He's lovely. But I didn't think things would last for this long. Or get so intense so quickly. You're basically living there when he's made it clear it can't go anywhere..."

"It's just easier to stay in the one place," I tried to explain. "It's not all that intense. We're just enjoying each other," I insisted, trying to convince myself as well as her.

"That's all well and good but don't you want someone you can spend time with without being terrified of being caught? Don't you want to go out to dinner? Or dancing? Have someone with you on your birthday?"

I couldn't deny her points. They were good ones. "I'm happy, okay?"

"Okay. If that's true, then I'm happy for you. That's all I want for you. I'm only scared that you'll be hurt."

I walked over to where she sat on her bed and hugged her. "You're a good friend," I said, needing her hug more than I knew.

"I'm okay," she answered, smiling.

"So, what have I missed? Are you in love with him yet?" Odessa launched into an explanation of all her time with Eti since I'd been gone. And, then asked me all about my Italy trip and my Hawaii trip, before finally we got into the party planning details. It was the perfect distraction from all the churning in my mind.

I decided to go with the Thai restaurant Eti and Odessa had recommended. They had a private dining room and a killer menu. And then we decided we'd send my parents back to the hotel we booked for them before we went out dancing for the night. A perfect evening. Without the one person I wanted to spend it with. Odessa invited Eti and a few of his friends, including Carter. I'd invited a few of my model friends and a friend from home, Tyler, who'd come to visit for his own reasons at the very convenient time.

Midway through the party planning, Brady texted me that he'd rushed out the door, realizing he was running late. I doubted it. Odessa and I spent the day playing catch up with each other since we hadn't spent a lot of time together since Brady came more firmly into the picture. As the evening rolled round and I realized I hadn't heard from Brady, I texted to ask if I should head over.

Brady: *Not tonight. I'll be working late. x*

* * *

With the whole next day to spare, Odessa and I shopped for dresses and shoes and clutches, and cute 20s style fur coats for the evening. To dissuade me from buying a necklace that went with my silver sparkly dress, Odessa admitted that her present was similar. Not wanting the day to end, and grateful for the gift though I hadn't yet seen it, I decided to buy us an afternoon of pampering. We got facials, massages, body scrubs, mani pedis, and then quick haircuts. Odessa's shaved head was refreshed, and I trimmed off the dead ends of my long locks. Still waiting to hear from Brady as we Ubered home, I shot off another text.

Haven: *Tonight?*

Brady: *A whole bunch of stuff has come up. I might need a few days.*

My stomach clenched.

"What's wrong?" Odessa asked, noticing my expression.

"Nothing," I said quickly. "Stomach ache."

"I'll make you some tea when we get home," Odessa said, taking my hand. I should've just been honest with her. I didn't reply to Brady.

We arrived home and Odessa made us both a pot of peppermint tea. My stomach was fine, but it soothed my heart a little. We watched *Peaky*

Blinders on Netflix until we couldn't keep our eyes open.

She woke me up the next day with the necklace. A simple silver chain with a droplet crystal on the end. "Odessa! Can you afford this?" I asked.

"I've been saving," she admitted.

I shook my head. She should not be spending her money on me. "I can't accept this."

"Of course you can. I insist you do," she said, kissing my cheek. "Happy birthday."

"Thank you," I said.

"We have to go get your parents in two hours," she reminded me.

"Yes," I said, jumping out of bed, preparing to get ready. I checked my phone quickly before jumping in the shower. I had a dozen birthday messages already. I sent a thank you and a kiss to them all and got into the shower.

Under the scalding stream of water, I realized I had heard nothing from Brady. He must've been busy. Maybe the shoot day started early. I pushed it to the back of my mind.

Odessa and I got an Uber to the airport, wanting to be there to greet my parents. They'd come to visit me in New York but hadn't had the chance to come to LA yet, even though it was closer. Odessa had made a pink sparkly sign for 'MR AND MRS ROSER' and we held it up at the arrival gate.

Mom and Dad came out early, with bright smiles on their faces. I rushed over to hug my dad first, and then my mother, taking their bags from them. Odessa took the other, greeting my parents lovingly. I knew she missed her own. "How was your flight?" I asked them as we walked out to get ourselves another Uber.

"I loved every second," my dad said. "Your mother fell asleep."

"It's just too comfortable. All planes should have flat laying beds. Not just in first class."

"Should be a human right, shouldn't it?" Odessa joked.

"It should," my mother said, seriously.

We went back to the hotel to drop their things. I'd booked them into the one across the street, Brady's favorite, and then brought them over to see Odessa's and my place. They were charmed. They gave me a gift, a variety of photo frames with pictures of us as family. Odessa had let them know that we didn't have many pictures around the house. It was the perfect gift.

We had ourselves some quick afternoon tea before my parents left to get ready for the dinner. Odessa and I did the same.

Odessa wore an olive colored silk midi dress and tall boots while I wore a silver sparkly thing with matching strappy sandals, going all out for the night. We wore our matching 20s style faux fur coats. Mine was black, hers was brown.

My parents met us outside. Mom had dressed in a red wrap dress, looking much younger than her 55 years and Dad wore a navy suit. We taxied to the restaurant where a group of a dozen people, Eti and Carter, my friends, my agent, were already there waiting. I made the rounds, introducing everyone to my parents, accepting an assortment of gifts, and finally took a seat at the head of the table in the private dining room. The restaurant served us an array of Thai dishes, curries, hot pots, stir fries - all of it delicious - alongside cocktails, wine, and a bottle of champagne to go with the cake that Odessa had chosen.

"Your friends are lovely, Haven," Mom said, taking my hand.

"I like Eti, Odessa," Dad said.

Odessa looked over to her beau who was leaving the room to have a smoke.

"Thanks, Mr. Roser," she answered. "I like him, too."

"Are you seeing anyone, Haven?" Mom asked.

"No," I said quickly, seeing Odessa's mouth open, ready to cause a little trouble.

"Why not?" She asked me. "There are some gorgeous men in this town."

Carter perked up in his seat, obviously catching part of our conversation.

"Just busy," I said. I realized again that I hadn't heard from Brady. Not a text or a call. No flowers delivered to the house. It hurt. It was a hurt I had been anticipating but I wasn't ready to feel it. I pushed it down.

I imagined him in Eti's empty chair. I imagined him impressing my dad the way Eti had. I knew my dad was only a few years older than him and it might've been weird at first, but I also knew Brady could win him over. With his intelligence and worldliness, and how he treated me. My mom might've been even more weirded out, knowing that he was on her walls in her youth. But if she knew how happy he made me... and he does, I thought, make me happy. Those three little words flashed again in my mind. I loved him. I knew it was soon, but I couldn't help the way I felt. It was undeniable. Where the hell was he?

We had cake next, a two-tier sponge cake covered in chocolate dipped strawberries. It was delicious but it didn't do anything to soak up the three cocktails I'd downed at dinner. I was tipsy and ready to dance. We sent my parents home and they discouraged any more drinking. We agreed, our fingers mentally crossed behind our backs, before heading to the selected club.

We were ushered in and taken to a VIP table, with bottle service and plush couches. Carter poured us all a round of shots and made a toast to me. "The incomparable Haven Roser."

We downed them and then made our way to the dance floor. At first, we were all dancing together but at some point, there was a partnering off. Eti was dancing with Odessa. My friend Tyler had hit it off with my model friend, Peter, and a couple of my girlfriends had found boys on the dance floor to grind against. Carter pulled me to him, naturally, and I allowed it. He was a good dancer, or at least the drunk version of me thought so.

We danced close, our skin touching, our sweat mingling. He turned me around, so my back was to him, his hands on my hips, as we swayed and dropped. I couldn't help but think of Brady, and the way he danced, the way I felt dancing with him, the sexy sensual beat of the song. The house music beats were different, dirtier. The club was dirty, too, the floor sticky, the air dense and smoky. He turned me back around and my brought my lips to him. No, I thought, keeping them away. But we kept dancing. He kept touching. And I touched back, the dancing my excuse.

We danced and drank and danced into the wee hours of the morning. Eti came back from a smoke to let us know there were paps outside. They were obviously there for Eti, but my minuscule amount of fame meant that they'd likely take a photograph of me, too. And, I was sure I looked terrible.

"Am I a mess?" I asked Carter, pushing my hair back from my sweaty head.

"No," he said. "Let me take you home."

"Okay," I agreed, not considering what he meant by those five casual words.

I kissed Odessa goodbye, she was going to Eti's. Carter half carried me out of the club and into his Uber, passing by a few paps who did indeed get our picture according to the aggressive flashing against my closed eyelids. He helped me from the car, into the apartment, even into my bed.

"You're sweet," I said, touching his arms where they'd brought my blanket up and over me.

"You're drunk," he said, having made his mind up not to take advantage of me I guessed.

"I still have my faculties," I answered.

"Oh yeah? Which ones?"

I ran my hands up his arms, over his shoulders, to his neck, I brought him close to me. In the dark, I could pretend he was Brady. I could pretend he'd come to see me, to wish me a happy birthday, to kiss me goodnight. I kissed him softly. I felt him smile against my lips.

"Happy birthday," he said, in a voice that sounded nothing like Brady's. "Good night."

I didn't say anything else as I heard him leave my room and then the apartment. I started to cry then, in the dark, drunk, sad, and sure that I didn't want to stay that way. There was so much good. I thought I'd die if I never had him inside me again, my mouth on his cock, his hands on my neck. To never laugh with him or watch Netflix by his side or ride around Malibu on the back of his Harley. I could make a thousand excuses. But if I could only have him in secret, then it wasn't enough for me. And, it had to be over.

BRADY

I wanted to call her, but the shoot began so early. And, Gaillard had made it clear a few days ago that his no phones on set rule applied to me as well. We shot through lunch, so I didn't have a chance then either. I called her around 8pm, when I got home from work, but she didn't answer. I called again at 9 and again at 10. Nothing. I didn't want to miss it. I didn't want her to think I hadn't called her on her birthday. I called again at 11 and sent a message asking her to call me back. Nothing. Eventually I fell asleep.

I woke up at 6am to my alarm and had no time to make the call then. I showered and changed and drove to set. They got me straight into hair and makeup. I waited until they left me alone to make the call. No answer, again. What the fuck?!

I took out my laptop, ready to answer some emails. One of the emails, from one of my producers, asked about Etienne Charpentier for a role. Odessa's boyfriend, I thought. I googled the kid. I looked over his IMDB, his Wikipedia. Then I clicked on news.

Etienne Charpentier and rumoured girlfriend go clubbing...

I clicked on the news link. I read a little and then just looked at the images. There were pictures of Etienne and Odessa leaving the restaurant they'd gone to for Haven's birthday. Then there was a picture of Haven. Holy shit, she looked good. She wore a sparkly dress that hugged her curves and lit up her skin. Her lips were painted a vibrant red. I took out my phone, ready to text that she looked beautiful.

I kept scrolling. There were pictures of Etienne and Odessa leaving a club, both looking a little worse for wear. And, then another picture of Haven. This one had Carter beside her, his arm wrapped around her, holding her up. Her eyes were closed. She looked wasted. Her lipstick was gone. What the fuck does that mean?

Then a picture of them getting into a taxi together.

Did she go home with him? Did she fuck him? I chucked my phone. I slammed the laptop closed. I stood up, walking out of the trailer and lighting a cigarette. Fuck!

HAVEN

I woke up at 11am and checked my phone. There they were four missed calls and a text. The first call was at 8pm. I thought I'd checked it after that and there had been nothing. But it didn't really matter. 8pm was late enough. I remembered Carter tucking me in. I remembered kissing him. I remembered how I'd spent the day in pain because Brady hadn't reached out. Because he was pulling away, that much was obvious. I remembered deciding that things had to be over between Brady and me.

Brady: *Work has been crazy today. I tried to get a hold of you but I'm sure you're out having a brilliant time. Happy Birthday. x*

Haven: *Can we talk tonight?*

I knew he was on set, which means no reply until lunch time. That would only be in an hour or so, I thought. But I didn't get a response until after 5pm. I did get a text from Carter.

Carter: *I had so much fun last night. When are you going to let me take your photo?*

Haven: *Soon x*

I waited around all day, trying to keep myself from going back on the determination I'd made. Brady's lack of reply helped a little. But my heart still ached. I wasn't sure if she was the angel or the devil, but something whispered to me to just deal with it. Have as much of him as you can for as long as you can. But things couldn't go on this way. The bad was starting to outweigh the good though I never would've believed it to be possible. For me, he was everything. I had started to feel like nothing to him. I started to feel like nothing at all. It wasn't okay. I deserved better.

Finally, the text arrived.

Brady: *Come over?*

Haven: *Be there soon.*

I got myself changed into something pretty, a summer midi dress and my combat boots. I ordered an Uber and went downstairs to wait for it. You never had to wait long in this town. Within the half hour I was at his door, using the key he'd given me to let myself in.

"Knock, knock," I called out.

"Here," he called back, sitting on a pool chair in the backyard. I walked over to find him sipping on a glass of whiskey. "There's one for you," he said, gesturing to the glass on the side table by the chair across from him. I took a seat, leaving the whiskey.

"How was your birthday?"

"Good. Fine." Not Happy Birthday? Not sorry I didn't call until too late? I was confused by his mood. I had come over to make something of an ultimatum, but he didn't know that. Still he was standoffish.

"You had fun?" he asked, downing the last of his drink.

"I did. I missed you," I said, trying to bring him back from whatever cloud he had over him. It was obviously not a good time to be making demands about us.

"Really? Didn't look like it." He reached past me and took the other glass. "If you're not going to drink this then I will." He started on the other glass.

"Didn't look like it?" I asked.

"I saw you come out of the club with Carter. All over him. And, then go home together. Did you fuck him?"

I coughed out half a laugh. "Are you serious right now?" He tilted his head a little, in faux-confusion. "He was at the party. We danced a little. He dropped me home in a taxi."

Brady nodded. "Did you kiss him?" I liked the other jealousy. The sweet jealousy. This was ugly.

"Why is that any of your business? We're just casually seeing each other here, aren't we? Until I find someone suitable? Wasn't that the big plan you laid out for me like I needed you to decide my life for me?"

Brady threw the glass, shattering it on the marble and sending splinters across the floor. I jumped a little.

"What the fuck?" I said quietly.

"I don't like him," Brady said, deciding his problem was with the one particular boy.

"You really don't have to like him, Brady."

I tried to calm down. I tried to remember how much I cared for him, to let that float over the anger. I had come here for a reason.

"I'm not okay with this anymore," I started.

"Okay with what?" He snapped back.

"The agreement. The secret."

"You know, you're right," he said, seeming to disregard the last thing I said. "Who cares what I think about Carter. He's age appropriate. He's not dealing with a divorce. He can be photographed holding your hand. Go be with him."

Now, he's pushing me away? "You're going about this all wrong."

"I have no idea what you're talking about," he spouted, walking inside and back to the bottle of whiskey on his counter. I followed him.

"You don't want this to be over," I declared, so sure of myself. He didn't answer me. He just started pouring another drink.

"Do you need that?" I asked. "I'm trying to talk to you."

"You can be such a fucking kid sometimes."

That was low. It made me go lower.

"Is this the side Cat got from you? Cause maybe I get why she kicked you out."

I felt the hit in the stomach like it was my own. Why did I say that? That was a horrible thing to say. I started to apologize but he spoke over me. "This has run its course, Haven."

"Brady," I started.

"You should go. Leave the key."

Just like that. He took his whiskey and went into his room and I was alone in the house I decorated holding a key in my shaky hand. I had so much more I wanted to say. Why did I have to fight back like that? I knew what he was going through. But why did he have to talk to me like I was a child? He'd never done that before, and I didn't know how to react. And now I'd got the complete opposite of what I wanted. We were over. Just like that.

I set the key down and started to walk away. Every footstep was louder than the last. I imagined him hearing me walk away from inside his room. I imagined him considering coming after me, but he didn't. I still had shoes at the door. I still had things all over the house. But I couldn't go get them. I felt frozen, only moving as little as I had to, to get out of that house and find a place to fall apart. I wanted to cry. I wanted to scream.

I wandered down his street to order an Uber. I didn't want to stay standing out the front of his house. It came quickly. I told myself I could fall apart at home.

I walked in the door and saw Odessa wasn't there. I went into my bedroom and sat down on the bed. I thought it would be the moment to cave in, but I couldn't bring myself to do it. I crawled up the bed and closed my eyes, letting myself sleep for a few hours. When I woke up, just before midnight, I was still there. Just far enough away from the breaking point. Instead of breaking, I picked up the skates from my floor and ran out.

✳ ✳ ✳

I hadn't been skating in weeks. It was the perfect time for it. I told myself, just skate. Forget it all for a few hours. Maybe you can outrun it. But a taxi, maybe the same one that took me home from Brady's, who knows, hit me as I crossed the road against a stop light.

As a kindly woman held me, I let it all out. I cried in her arms. I cried like I'd been needing to.

Paramedics helped me into their ambulance, but I knew I was okay. I didn't want to go to the hospital. I asked to be allowed to go and although they advised against it, they released me. I got into another taxi, which felt off but necessary, and took myself home.

I arrived back in the apartment to find Odessa sleeping soundly in her bed. I climbed in beside her, not wanting to be alone, and woke to find me there, snuggling into her back.

"Hi friend," she said, a little surprised. "What are you doing home?"

"Brady ended it," I said, quietly.

She gasped a little and turned around slowly to face me. "Why?"

"I don't know," I said. I really didn't understand what had happened at all.

"I'm so sorry," she said, taking my hand and bringing it to her heart.

I didn't have any excuse this time. I started crying again. I felt pitiful. Odessa put a comforting hand on my back, rubbing gently. She asked me questions and I tried to answer them, I tried to explain as best I could, but Odessa didn't seem to understand it either. When I couldn't speak anymore, she just whispered softly. "It'll be okay. You'll be okay."

I fell asleep to those quiet words with my own inner voice echoing back. No. No, it won't.

BRADY

I don't know what happened. I just saw her and snapped. I couldn't get the image of her and Carter out of my mind. And, I hated myself for wanting to deny her the thing I knew was necessary. It was never going to work with us, so she needed to be unavailable to me. But I couldn't bear the thought of it. It had only been six weeks. Six weeks, but I dreaded being without her. It felt like ripping myself apart to end it, but I feared how much worse it would be if I let it go on any longer.

"Is this the side Cat got from you? Cause I get why she kicked you out." Those words echoed in my mind as I listened to her footsteps walking out of my life. It was brutal. I'd never heard her say anything so cruel. And yet, I knew I deserved it. I'd had two glasses before she'd arrived and another two right there in front of her. I was trying to go numb, but she was too vibrant, the energy between us too loud to be numbed quiet. Even while she was standing there, hating me I was sure, I knew I'd never want anyone the way I wanted her. In my home, in my bed, in my life.

Maybe I would've changed my mind. If Catalina hadn't called in the very next day. I thought she was dropping the girls, but she'd left them with her brother.

"I need to speak to you," she said, dropping her heavy handbag with a thud. She wanted her hands empty so she could gesture as wildly as possible. She had points to make.

"I know who you're dating," she said, as I walked toward the kitchen to get her a drink. I turned back around quickly.

"What are you talking about?"

"I heard she's a kid. 20 years old." I could see the steam coming from her ears. My heart beat faster. This was what I'd feared.

"Who told you that?" I demanded. There were so few people who knew. I racked my mind. I was going to kill them.

"What does it matter? Is it true? Are you fucking a kid?" Her hands curled into fists.

"No. Not anymore," I said, plainly. I needed to deescalate.

"Are you kidding me? Mannix is 16! She's practically the same age." Her eyes were wide as saucers, her voice was getting louder and louder.

I lifted my hands defensively. "Listen. Please calm down. She's 23."

"23?" she spat. "You listen to me. That girl is not getting anywhere near my kids. Do you understand me? I will sue for full custody and I will win because that is fucking sick."

"Cat, please, calm down for a second. Let me get you a drink." I started back to the kitchen.

"I don't want a fucking drink," she said and started back to the door. I rushed after her.

"It's over. It's over now," I said, turning her around, touching her elbows. It was the most I'd touched her in a year.

She shook me off. "It's over?"

"Yes. We broke up. A while ago," I lied. "She's gone."

"I'm disgusted."

I took it, as long as she believed it was over, I'd be okay. I'd be allowed to see my kids. "I'm sorry," I said.

She nodded, calming, her breathing steadying.

"Please don't threaten me again," I said. "I have a right to see my kids."

"No, you don't," she pushed me back with her palms flat on my chest. "Not if some child bride is here with you. Absolutely not. And any judge would agree with me. A 20-year-old. They'd think you were having some kind of midlife crisis. You know what men do in a midlife crisis? They murder their families."

"Jesus Christ! What the hell is wrong with you?" I didn't recognize this person. Who could say something so horrific? She knew I could never be capable of something like that.

"What the hell is wrong with you!" she yelled back, pushing me again.

"Don't push me," I said, quietly.

"Is that a threat?" she snapped back.

"No. Don't physically push me," I answered.

She crossed her arms appearing in the smallest way chastened.

I took a breath. "Listen, I'm sorry our marriage ended. I'm sorry you were so unhappy and I'm sorry I didn't know how to fix it. But I love our kids. I love them so much and I want to be in their lives, as much as I would if we had stayed together."

"I'm not stopping you," she said. "Not if you're alone."

"So, I have to be alone forever?"

"Not forever. Just not with a fucking teenager. Do you understand me? There is no way." I knew all this. I knew it. It felt like hammering a nail into the coffin that carried all my possible happiness with the girl I... What did it matter now?

"I understand," I said.

She started back to her bag, picking it up and heading for the door.

"Wait," I said, following her. I held the door as she stepped out.

"I have a meeting," she claimed.

"I want to see Mannix," I said.

"He's 16. He makes his own decisions," she insisted.

I nodded. "I know. I can't force him. But I can't even talk to him about any of this. I can't imagine what he thinks of me. If you could encourage him maybe. To call me. To give me a chance to beg to be in his life. I'll beg if I have to. Tell him I love him."

Cat started to nod. There was barely any emotion on her face. It had been anger or nothing at all. "I'll try," she said finally. "Goodbye."

"Bye," I said quietly as she walked back to her Escalade. I closed the door behind her and fell back against it, sliding down the wooden panels and onto the marble floor. I held my head in my hands, squeezing tightly to quell the rage.

HAVEN

I showed up to his door at 9pm, days after he'd kicked me out. I didn't tell Odessa was going. I could barely admit it to myself as I Ubered over. But I had to try. I had to.

I buzzed twice when he answered. He could see me. He wasn't happy to. His voice said it all.

"What are you doing here, Haven?"

"Can I come in?" I asked.

"I don't think that's a good idea."

I stilled at that. "There are things I need to say."

"I think you should go." He won't even let me in. I second guessed myself, but I had things to say and I couldn't leave without saying them.

"I want you to change your mind," I said. "I realized something these last few days. I realized I'd been searching for a sense of purpose. Like my mom always wanted me to. I've been searching all along without really thinking about it. I thought I would find some purpose in all the chaos of New York. I thought that traveling the world would open me up to all its possibilities, but I found no passion for anything. Until you."

He said nothing. Was he even there listening? I kept going.

"Not modeling. Not any of the guys I ever dated. There was no place, no thing, no person. I never fixated on anything. I never wanted anything… so much as you."

I waited there as the minutes passed. Finally, he spoke. "I can't be your passion, Haven. It can't be me."

"Why not?" I said, my voice breaking, wanting to cry. "Why the hell not?"

Nothing again. I watched as a car passed by, the driver looking out his window to me.

"Just let me in," I pleaded, the same way I had all those weeks before. "Let me in."

"We had a good run, didn't we?" His voice had changed, become harder, less recognizable. "You knew it wasn't going to last."

I knew that's what he said. But deep down I hadn't let myself believe it. I thought everything I was feeling was reciprocated and one day he'd wake up and realize I'm the girl for him, age gap or none, and we should be together. It just never happened. And, I felt like a fool.

"I'm sorry," I said, in lieu of a goodbye. I walked away.

I walked home, not bothering with a taxi or Uber. My mind was too full to mind the distance or the pain of my toes, my shoes half a size too small.

I kept going over and over every inch of memories and agonizing over the truth of them, so scared that I'd made it all up in my head. No, I assured myself. It happened and it was great and now it was over. I had to move forward with my life. There was so much left to live. I just hated the thought of living it without him.

CHAPTER TEN:
A night to remember...

BRADY

I hadn't spoken to her in weeks. But I couldn't keep from looking her up, seeing if she'd been out and about. With Carter. Or anyone. She hadn't as far as I'd seen. I did my best to keep my mind from her. Especially at work. But if anything, I was even more distracted. Maybe I hid it better. I kept my phone off. But my mind still wandered.

At lunch, watching the previous day's footage with Gaillard, I was thinking of Haven, of the way she laughed at the stupid things I did, the way she made me laugh, when the producer came into the trailer in a huff. "We have a problem," he said.

"Don't tell me that," Gaillard said.

"Shani's mother got into a car accident. She's in a coma. Shani's flying home tomorrow."

"Shit," Gaillard said.

Shani was playing a small but important part and was supposed to shoot her scenes over the next two days.

"Who else is available?" Gaillard asked.

"With a shaved head or willing to shave it? Not a lot of options. I'm getting the old auditions re-emailed."

"Fuck," Gaillard said, pausing the dailies and getting out his phone.

Shaved head. I knew who could play that part. Haven had shown me some of Odessa's work. I knew she had talent. She just hadn't had the right opportunity, the right luck.

"Gaillard," I said, "I know someone."

"You do?"

"Her name is Odessa. Her head is shaved, bleached blonde, at least it was when I saw her last. She's good."

"What's she been in?"

"Nothing yet," I admitted. "She's had some shit luck."

"Anything I can watch?" He asked.

"I can send her the script. Get her to put something on tape."

"In the next hour?" He asked.

I nodded. "It shouldn't be a problem."

"Okay," he said. "Do it."

I stepped out of the trailer and turned my phone back on. I didn't have Odessa's number. I didn't know how Haven would feel about me reaching out for this reason, but I had to now.

Brady: *Hey Haven, Sorry to bother you but can I grab Odessa's number? We might have a part for her.*

Her texts came back quickly. First Odessa's contact details. And then...

Haven: *Thanks for thinking of her.*

Of course, she didn't have any thought for herself. Just for Odessa.

I called Odessa. She answered excitedly.

"Hi," she said.

"Hey Odessa. Have you spoken to Haven?"

"I have. She's right here."

"Good. I'm sending you the script now," I said, putting her on speaker and finding it in my emails. "Gaillard wants you to put something on tape within the hour if you can."

"I can," she said.

"Great. Just email it to me."

"Okay. Brady?"

"Yeah?"

"Thank you," she said, her tone genuinely grateful.

"You're welcome."

Within the hour - she used almost all of it, preparing I guessed - she'd sent the tape. Gaillard was with me when it came through and we stepped back into the trailer to watch it.

Odessa read with Haven behind the camera. Hearing her voice was distracting. I tried to focus on Odessa. She was good. Of course, she was. Better than I remembered. Midway through Gaillard nudged me, obviously pleased. When it was over, he clapped. "Good man," he said. "Let's book her."

I sent her the text.

Brady: *You got it. You'll get your call sheet soon. You're on tomorrow.*

Odessa: *Holy shit. Thank you!*

Brady: *It was all you. See you tomorrow.*

HAVEN

My mind had never been so occupied during a shoot. I knew Odessa was on set with Brady and it was all I could think about while I was shooting the watch campaign that he'd turned down.

When he asked for Odessa's number so she could audition for Gaillard Trentino, I helped her record an audition tape. She sent it off and within twenty minutes she was cast. It was the moment she'd been waiting for. She'd worked hard and she deserved it. She promised she'd only be as nice as was necessary to Brady, but I knew how grateful she was. I was grateful, too. As mad as I was, as sad as I was, he did something pretty amazing. And, now she was there, with him, looking at him, talking to him, and I wished I had taken up acting instead of modeling.

My day's co-star was Trevor Rhoda, a seriously good-looking black man with the broadest shoulders I'd ever seen. He could tell my mind was elsewhere.

"What's going on?" He asked me.

"I'm sorry," I said. "I'm not usually like this."

"I figured. Is everything okay?"

"It's okay," I said.

"You sure?"

"Yes." This was unprofessional. I had to get my shit together. There was nothing I could do there. I knew Odessa would tell me everything when she got home in the evening. I was determined to focus and get on with the shoot. They had us laying awkwardly side by side in a bed.

"Trev," called the photographer. "Can you sit up, touch her cheek?"

"May I?" He asked.

I nodded. He turned onto his side and leaned over me, his arm rested on my chest, his hand, watch on the wrist, went to my cheek. I brought my hand up and touched it lovingly, showing off my watch.

"That's great."

At the end of the shoot, as we were saying goodbye, Trevor asked if I was single.

"I am," I answered.

"Could I maybe get your number?" He asked.

"Oh," it was a little out of left field. He hadn't spoken much through the shoot. I had no idea he was interested. "Okay," I said, because why shouldn't I? He was handsome and single and dating was something I should probably do. Even if only to distract me from the endless stream of thoughts about *him*.

BRADY

I saw Odessa as she arrived, delivered by one of the assistant directors to hair and makeup. I read my sides as I waited for her to come out, nervous about what she'd say. I didn't doubt that she'd be grateful, but I wondered what she might feel on Haven's behalf. I imagined Haven had told her everything. How I had gotten drunk and ended things. The glass I'd thrown, like a fucking cowardly idiot. How I'd left that sweet girl standing outside my house, pouring her heart into a speaker box. I wanted to know how she was. I wanted to know if she was dating that fucking Carter or anyone else. Would Odessa even be willing to talk to me about her?

Finally, she came out. Gaillard went to greet her, praising her audition tape, and complimenting how she looked in the costume. She was slightly smaller than Shani, so they had to make some quick alterations.

"Well, it looks brilliant. We're so grateful you could make it at the last minute," Gaillard continued.

"Please," Odessa said. "I'm the one who's grateful for the opportunity."

"Well give us a sec, feel free to order a coffee. Brady's just over there." Odessa looked at me, she smiled a little, close mouthed. Then she approached.

"Hey," she said, as we hugged somewhat awkwardly.

"How are you?"

"Good. Thank you again for this."

"Of course. You deserve it," I said.

We stood awkwardly for a little while. An assistant asked if Odessa wanted a coffee and she ordered an iced latte. I had a cappuccino in hand. I had a million questions but no courage to ask them.

"You haven't been around," she started.

"Yeah," I sighed.

"What the hell happened?"

"You don't know?" I asked, sure from the way she was glaring at me that she did.

"She tried to explain it, but it sounded like a load of bullshit to me." She definitely spoke her mind.

I nodded. I definitely wasn't going to argue with her about it. But there was one thing I had to know.

"Is she with Carter?"

"What?" Odessa asked, her brows furrowed, her mouth wide.

"Carter Rousey? The kid with the dark hair..."

"I know who he is," she said. "They're not dating."

"Oh. It was just a one-time thing?"

"No. They were never... why would you think--"

I cast my mind back to the pictures. "On her birthday there were pictures of him all over her."

"Oh my god. No. She was drunk. He just helped her home," she explained.

"Oh," I said, not sure if I could believe it.

"She's not seeing anyone actually. Still pining over you. Not sure why cause dumping her like that was a dick move. I know I probably shouldn't be having a go at you when you've done this for me, but she is still my best friend and I'm already here so fuck it," she said. Her coffee came back, and she had a sip. Her eyebrows furrowed deeper and she looked at the brew. "This is great coffee."

"Yeah, they get the good stuff," I said, my mind still processing the rest of it. "So, she's not... seeing anyone."

"I really shouldn't have said anything," she said, a little nervous. "But, is that why you dumped her? You thought she was with Carter?"

"No. No. There are a lot of reasons why it just wasn't going to work."

"So, it was pre-emptive?" she scoffed. "Good one."

She was laughing at me. I could take it. She didn't know the situation. Even Haven didn't know the full extent of the situation. Maybe that was the problem. I had thought that ending it swiftly, without much talk or fanfare, was the right thing. Or I was deluding myself into thinking that because I couldn't face her. She did deserve an explanation. But so much time had already passed.

We were over. It was done. No point winding the wheel back. Maybe I'd hurt her by ending things the way I did, but they needed to be over. She was too young for me. It wouldn't be good for either of us. The reasons were still the same. I just needed the reminder. This was the right thing. "Just believe me," I started. "This is for the best."

"Wow," Odessa said then, looking at me like the coward I was. "Okay."

"Odessa!" Gaillard called. She put on a smile, set down her coffee and went over to our director to start blocking the scene. "Brady," he called me next. I followed.

HAVEN

I didn't want to sit at home waiting for Odessa only for her to tell me that she had nothing to tell me. Or maybe she'd have something to tell and it would just fucking kill. No. I was a woman of action. And, action was just what I needed. Trevor had texted me earlier to make sure I had his number. I shot off a text in reply.

Trevor: *This is Trevor*

Haven: *Hey, Trevor, what are you doing right now?*

Trevor: *Hey, quiet girl. Not much.*

Haven: *You wanna come over?*

Trevor: *What's your addy?*

I sent over my address and he showed within the half hour. I had cleaned the apartment, tidied up my room, and ran out to buy a bottle of the nearest liquor store's finest vodka. I had just poured two glasses by the time he arrived. He knocked gently on the door and I made my way over, straightening my t-shirt dress and brushing my hair back from my face.

Trevor's lips curled into an o as he looked me up and down.

"Come in," I said, stepping aside. He walked through with a swagger that I hadn't noticed before. His scent came by me. He smelled like sandalwood aftershave and toothpaste.

He was massively built, like training for two hours every morning kind of built. He wore a maroon t-shirt with gold rimmed black ray bans tucked into his collar and a pair of blue jeans half tucked into Timberlands.

He looked around at my apartment, appraising it. "What do you think?" I asked.

"You live here alone?"

"I have a roommate but she's out for the night." As far as I knew.

"What do you got there?" he asked, looking at the glasses poured out.

"Vodka," I answered, walking into the kitchen and handing one over.

"Vodka and what?" he asked.

"Ice," I answered, and he laughed.

I came back around the kitchen island and we clinked our glasses before taking a sip. I took more than a sip and Trevor eyed me curiously.

"So, what is it?" he asked.

"What's what? Do you wanna sit?"

We took spots on the couch across from each other.

"What's up with you?" he asked.

I took another great gulp of the vodka and then set it aside before climbing up onto my knees and moving over to him. He watched me come, his eyes running up from my thighs as I lifted the t-shirt dress up and over my head. I had nothing underneath and his eyes widened. He reached out for me, his hands soft and warm on my cold skin.

"It's like that?" he asked. Simple as that.

I nodded as I climbed into his lap, my hands on his broad rounded shoulders. I looked into his eyes. They were kind eyes, black where Brady's were blue, but kind. I leaned down and kissed him. I wanted to cry. But I kept going. His lips were big and soft and able. He opened up to me and his tongue came to meet mine.

I let my hands travel down to grab the edge of his shirt, bringing it up and over his head, breaking our kiss. My fingers ran over his bulging abs, up his prominent chest, and back to his neck. I kissed him again, deeper, hungrier and he met me want for want. He started dominating our kiss and I let him, letting him swallow my lips in his, and kissing them raw as I worked to unbuckle his belt and then his jeans before we pushed them down together and away.

I could feel his hard-on then; his soft cotton briefs the only thing between us. I touched him through the cotton. He was massive and straining toward me. I shifted up and onto him, grinding into him.

As I got my breath, Trevor licked and sucked down my neck and onto my chest, taking my nipples one at time into his mouth, flicking them with his tongue and sucking them. As my eyes closed at the sensation, I couldn't stop my mind from picturing Brady. His head between my chest, his tongue on my skin, his strong hands holding me over him, his cock beginning to gently thrust at my core and the annoying barrier between us.

I ran my hand over his shaved head. Brady had never shaved his head with me. But he'd had a shaved head over the years. I could even pretend it was his head I was holding onto. I could pretend it was his fingers spreading me open, plunging into me curiously.

I moaned a little, bounced a little, before grabbing for his briefs to drag them down.

Trevor grabbed at my cheeks, bringing my face back to him. I was forced to open my eyes.

"Where are you?" he asked.

"Huh?" I said, a little breathless.

"You sure as hell ain't here with me. You using me?"

"What?"

He brushed the fallen locks away from my eyes. "You thinking of someone else? Trying to get back at him? Is that what this is?"

I bit my lip and nodded. "Trying to forget him. Is that okay?"

He considered a moment, even looked down at my naked torso, weighing it up.

"Yeah, I'll be that for you."

I pushed back into him, closing my eyes and taking his lips. He pushed me back, taking us over onto my back.

I spread my legs and he nestled between us. "Condom?" I asked as I took him in my hands, pumping up and down.

He groaned a little and then reached over to his discarded jeans. He took his wallet from his pocket, finding a foil packet in with the cash. He ripped open the condom and rolled it on to his thick black cock.

"Okay," I said, grabbing at his waist.

He positioned up and pushed into me. I cried out a little and closed my eyes again.

Brady, I said in my mind. Brady. Brady. Brady. It didn't feel exactly right. We didn't fit the same. He didn't taste the same. My skin didn't alight at his touch. But I could pretend.

"Put your hand around my neck," I whispered, reaching out for it.

"What?"

"Around my neck," I said, "please."

He seemed to consider it and slowly put his hand there, touching my skin and not much else.

"Tighter," I said, putting my hand on top of his and pressing down.

"No," He said.

"I like it," I said, opening my eyes again. "I like it," I repeated trying to assure him.

He squeezed a little and I closed my eyes. "Like that," I said. "Harder."

"I can't do this."

His hand came away "What? Why?" My eyes snapped back open. He pulled out of me and backed off, so quickly.

"You need to get your head right." He started dressing and I curled up into a ball, trying to cover myself up.

I scoffed. My head is fine, I wanted to say. But it wouldn't be true.

"I'm going to go," he said, handing me my dress from the floor. He started for the door.

"I'm sorry," I said quickly before I lost my chance.

He nodded once and then walked out. I pulled on my shirt and picked up the vodka with a shaky hand. I downed it and then his. I felt so scared. I didn't even know why. I felt cold and scared. I got up and ran myself a bath in the teeny bathroom Odessa and I shared. I didn't think it had ever been used by either of us.

I climbed in before it had even been a quarter filled, taking my vodka with me. I sat as deep into the tub as I could, covering myself with as much of the scalding water as I could. I sipped at my vodka with closed eyes and played the supercut of Brady and I to the sound of the rushing water. My skin pulsed with the violent hot heat of the water. I pressed the vodka glass into my cheek and enjoyed the cool.

I didn't know what this was, but it didn't feel like getting through it. It felt like a slow and spectacular disaster.

✳ ✳ ✳

Gaillard loved Odessa, of course, because she was brilliant, and she finally got the chance to show someone. She didn't have anything to report on Brady after her days on set and I didn't press. If she didn't want to say anything, I could guess it was because it wasn't anything I'd want to hear.

I didn't tell her about Trevor. Mostly because I wanted to pretend it never happened.

She told me everything about the shoot that didn't include Brady. How easily she'd relaxed into the part. How comfortable she felt in front of the cast and crew and Gaillard. In front of the camera was where she'd always belonged and now, she knew for sure. And, her career was about to take off.

Richard Rodriguez was looking for the star of his next film, the story of a Rihanna-type pop star who is kidnapped and fights her way out like a badass. Odessa was perfect for it and Gaillard recommended her. She auditioned just once and got the role. It was all happening for her. That lead role got her enough attention in Hollywood, as well as being Eti's girlfriend, that she was asked to present at the Golden Globes in place of someone who had dropped out. Eti was invited in his own right. Odessa asked me to be her date.

Brady had been nominated for a film he had produced. So, I knew he'd be there. I was sure it would be painful to see him. I'd been mourning the breakup as if we'd been a couple. But at the same time, I wanted to see him again. I'd probably always want to see him. I wanted to know what the hell happened between us. And, I wanted to support Odessa. I agreed to go.

I had reached out to a stylist I knew, who had dressed me for events in the past. She came over with rack upon rack of dresses and Odessa and I spent hours trying things on. I found two I liked pretty quickly. One red, lacy, very romantic. The other black, a bit more edgy and dramatic. I wasn't sure how I'd feel on the night, so we accessorised both and kept them on hold. Odessa took a little longer. She was going to be on stage, so it was understandable that she'd be careful about choosing the right one. I tried to give my most honest and discerning opinion, but she was so beautiful that she looked amazing in everything. It was Eti's opinion that she listened to after sending pictures of every dress to him. She chose a gold dress, sparkly and fitted, and very sexy. It wasn't a surprising choice from Eti.

On the day, I went with black. It was the sexier dress. And, if I saw the person I wanted to see then sexy was the best option. We had hair and makeup artists come to get us glammed up and a town car took us from the apartment to the show. We walked the carpet, our hands clasped, basking in the attention of the photographers and fans who knew my name and Odessa's already, too. I tried not to make it obvious as I looked for Brady on the red carpet.

We were about to walk into the lobby, where a crowd waited to be taken to their tables, when I felt a hand on my back. I turned around, coming face to face with Brady. He wore an immaculate tux. His beard was longer. Were his eyes bluer? My knees were weak. "Hi," I said. He leaned in to kiss me on the cheek. I closed my eyes, savoring it.

"Brady," Odessa said, accepting a kiss from him, too.

"Brady! Odessa! Can we get a picture?"

I stepped back. Brady and Odessa took their photo and then came back to me. Odessa looked between us and seemed to think we had something to say. "I'm just gonna... I'll be inside."

I watched her go. I crossed my arms a little, needing my own comfort as Brady looked down at me. He suddenly felt so tall. And, I so small.

"How are you?" He said, casually, like we were just old friends. Acquaintances.

"Fantastic," I said, glibly. "How are you?"

"Yeah good." Yeah good? He was good. He was great. He wasn't affected at all.

"Well, I should..." I started to turn. He reached out for my hand, but a few loud bright flashes made him flinch and he brought it back to his side. That was about right, I thought. It shouldn't have hurt so much.

"Have a good night," I said, the only four words I could manage and rushed inside to find Odessa.

BRADY

I almost took her hand. Right there in front of dozens of cameras and screaming fans. What a fucking idiot. She was just so beautiful, in her tight black dress. She looked like those old Hollywood icons I'd always compared her to. But I hated the way she was looking at me. Coldly. Closed off. Hard. She'd always been so soft. Strong, and occasionally sassy but mostly, soft. Sweet. Maybe it was too soon to see her. It had been two months since I'd last seen her. Not that I was counting.

I followed her into the lobby, but she was already gone. I was approached by an attendant and taken to my table. In the room, I kept looking for her. Would we be seated close by? Would we have any chance to talk? I realized I wanted to have the talk. She deserved it. I didn't want her to hate me. Maybe a bit of closure would help us both.

I took my seat, at a table with my fellow producers, the director and actors from the film I'd produced, the one we were nominated for. The group was already a few drinks in, celebrating the nomination. We weren't the front runner to win, so there was no reason to stay sober. I talked to the director but kept up my search.

"Who you looking for?" he asked eventually.

"Just a friend," I said.

He nodded and left me to it. She must've been sitting up close, because Odessa was presenting. Finally, I saw her, at a table toward the back of the lower level, maybe six or seven tables away from me, with a bunch of actors I knew and admired. Odessa was the life of the party, talking and laughing. Rachel Leigh, last year's winner for Best Actress, was speaking quietly with Haven. They seemed to be getting on.

At each ad break I got out of my chair and tried to make my way to her. Every time, without exception, I was accosted. By a friend or by a stranger who wanted to say hello, every single time. She didn't get up once, I noticed, but she was approached. By a few women, and a couple of guys, Etienne Charpentier too, who I guessed was saying hello to his girlfriend. She didn't look my way once. Her mood seemed to be improving and maybe that was why. She was pretending I wasn't there. It only made me want to talk to her more.

Finally, both she and Odessa got up and walked out of the room. I followed them both, excusing myself from those who wanted to chat. I reached the door of the lobby and saw Odessa being taken away, I guessed she was about to present. Haven walked to the bathroom. Shit. Well I'd wait, I thought. I walked toward the bar and got myself a beer, wanting something in my hands, a reason for being there. I waited a minute or two and then worried she might find another way back to her seat. I started toward the bathroom but was accosted again.

Charlie Torrance, a supermodel turned actress, grabbed my arm, leaned in to kiss my cheek and started raving about the film that was nominated.

"It had me bawling, I swear to god. How did you find your lead? He was unbelievable for his age. I was so shocked he wasn't nominated—"

I had to cut her off. "Thank you, Charlie. But I really have to go."

"Where do you have to go? Talk to me for a second. I never see you at these things—"

"I'll be back," I said, hoping that would sedate her.

She grabbed hold of my lapels. "You look so good. You wear a suit better than most, you know that? And, what is that smell?" She leaned in and pressed her nose to my neck. She was beautiful with short cropped red hair and a long elegant neck. Tough. Age appropriate. Interested. But I was praying she would walk away. Just as I was thinking how horrifying it would be for Haven to walk out in that moment and see this sight....

HAVEN

I wanted to be sick. Charlie Torrance was draped over Brady, kissing his neck. He was holding her arms, laughing at whatever she'd whispered to him in their little corner.

At least I knew now why he'd ended things so abruptly. She was beautiful. Tall. Thin. His age, or close enough to it. It made perfect sense. It fucking killed. I couldn't look at it a second longer. I rushed through the next door that opened, back into the auditorium.

CHAPTER ELEVEN:
Stay gold, Ponyboy!

HAVEN

"Haven!" I heard his voice calling behind me.

I got into my seat and sat still, trying to calm my breathing, praying he wouldn't approach. But he did. He put a hand on the back of my chair, the other on the table in front of me and leaned in.

"Haven, I need to talk to you," he said, quietly.

"How's it going, mate?" Rachel's husband said, holding a hand out to shake.

Brady shook it. "Good, Dan. Hi, Rachel."

"Hi," she said, obviously confused, eyeing the both of us.

"Haven?" He said again.

"It's really okay. We're good. We weren't anything..." Trying to pretend I wasn't about to fall apart. "We're good."

"Can we just talk for a second?"

"Ladies and gentlemen, if you'll please return to your seats..."

The host was coming back on. Brady reluctantly left our table and returned his seat.

"Are you okay? Haven?" Rachel asked.

"Yeah," I said, shrugging, like nothing at all had happened. She didn't look like she believed me. It was kind of her to care at all. "Thank you."

She nodded and smiled. The show went on. I watched as my best friend took the stage, focusing on her and her success. I screamed out for her and she eyed me with a smile from behind the microphone as her co-presenter spoke. She presented her award and got off the stage. She wouldn't be coming back to her seat since it was the last segment. I'd meet her in the lobby.

There were two more awards before the big one 'Best Picture.' Brady didn't win. We cheered for the winner and dutifully listened to his speech before we were able to stand. Most people started mingling, as they had in the ad breaks, before leaving the auditorium. I saw Brady leave his seat and try to come back to my table. No. No, I thought. I didn't want to talk to him. I didn't want to hear any kind of explanation. He didn't owe it to me, and I didn't want it. I rushed up the aisle to the lobby.

He didn't call out. I figured he'd given up. But as I searched the lobby for Odessa, he grabbed me by the arm and turned me around. "Haven, can you stop? For fuck's sake."

He was annoyed. Well I had run away from him twice now, so maybe it was understandable. "What?" I asked. What was he so desperate to say?

"I just want to talk to you," he answered.

"Here?" I asked, feigning shock. "In front of everyone? Wouldn't that harm your perfectly crafted image?"

He seemed to disregard my sarcastic question. "I just need you to know I'm not with her."

He's not? "You're not?"

"No. She just grabbed onto me. I tried to get her off—"

BRADY

"Okay," she said, cutting me off. "Why do I need to know that? You obviously don't give a shit about me."

"I—"

She cut me off again, seeming to change her mind about her anger. "I'm sorry. I have no right to be mad. We weren't a thing."

"Will you stop saying that?" I asked, surprising myself by how much it bothered me.

"What?" She asked, confused.

"That we were nothing. We were something."

"We were?" She asked with something like hope in her voice.

I had to admit it. To her and to myself. "I care about you. A lot."

"You do?" She asked, smiling just a little, her expression vulnerable, finally open. She reached a hand up, as if to run it through my hair. As I watched it go, I noticed all the eyes on us. It had felt like it was just us, but we were in the middle of a crowded room. Amongst all the people I feared knowing about us. And, I flinched again. And she saw it, again. She looked like she might cry.

She swallowed and spoke quietly. I could still feel the eyes on us, people standing nearby pretending to be listening to their own conversations, but instead listening to us. "Why can't we be together?"

"My kids…"

"Maybe she'd be okay with it. I could meet her," she suggested, her heart so willing to believe the best in people. But I looked around the vultures were everywhere.

"Everyone will judge us."

"Why do you give a shit?" She asked me. "I don't give a shit. I want them to know. I want to tell everyone."

She was so young, I thought again. For the millionth time. "You think you'd be fine. But you have no idea how something like this would damage your reputation. It would affect everything. It would follow you around forever."

"I don't care. I love you."

The words just fell out of her mouth. She seemed just as shocked to say them as I was to hear them. "What?" I said, stupidly. It was all I could think of to say.

And, then, with purpose. She repeated those three words. "I love you."

HAVEN

"Jesus, Haven," he said. It sounded like pity. Like I was a child he was berating. That was it then, I thought.

"I'm not a child," I said, fiercely. He seemed to feel the change in me.

"I know that," he said.

"No, you don't. You'll never see me as I am. As a woman. As the women in love with you."

"I—"

I cut him off, speaking as I was realizing; "This is useless. Any fight, any hope, is useless. I'm done."

He looked confounded. I felt empty.

"Goodbye, Brady," I said, walking away from him. I held my head high. I wouldn't cry there in front of him, I told myself. Or any of them. I'd go home and cry. And then I'd wake up and be done with it. No more thinking of him. Definitely no more crying over him. I'd work. I'd date. I'd move on.

I had to.

CHAPTER TWELVE: Forgetting him was like ...

HAVEN

Odessa took me home and held me as I cried for at least two hours before we both went to sleep. When I woke up in the morning, and wanted to start crying again, I stopped myself. I remembered the promise I'd made. That I was going to give myself that night and then I was going to move on.

I looked at my puffy red eyes in the mirror, the makeup caked into my skin, my hair a haystack. I hated the way I felt last night, I thought, and I hated that I still felt so hurt over him. That he didn't love me. That he couldn't see past my age. That he didn't believe Catalina could. That he didn't want to even try.

I also felt guilty for keeping Odessa from her after parties. They were more opportunities to network, and I ruined that with my hysterics. Well, I was done. I wasn't letting my personal drama affect her. Or me for that matter.

Fashion week came at the perfect time. I had booked dozens of shows and shoots. I made myself available for all social activities as well. After parties and nights out and lunches and breakfasts. I kept so busy. It was tiring. But worth it to have such an occupied mind. I could convince myself that I barely thought of him.

My last event was in Paris, a La Perla party. The room was a little too full of sycophantic people preening for the photographers covering the event and drinking excessively.

I was featured in a lot of their campaigns and so pictures of me, blown up to life size, were covering the room. Everywhere I looked I could see myself and in only lingerie. It was all a little overwhelming. I excused myself to take some air outside.

"Excuse me," a quiet accented voice sounded behind me.

I turned around to see a man leaning against the buildings, an unlit cigarette hanging from his lips.

"Do you happen to have a lighter?" He asked. His voice was a little coarse but warm.

"No," I said, apologetically.

He sighed as he removed the cigarette and returned it to the packet in his hand. "Thank you anyway."

"They'd probably have matches at the bar," I suggested.

He stepped away from the wall of the building and into the street light. I recognised his face. He was the Belgian actor, Luc Van den Bossche. I'd seen a few of his movies. He was brilliant. And extremely good looking.

"I don't really want to go back in there," he said.

I laughed a little. "Yeah, it's a little much."

"No," he said then, with a small smile. "I'd just rather talk to you."

"Oh." I blushed. I held out a hand for him to shake. "I'm Haven Roser."

"I know who you are," he said. "You're all over the walls in there."

"I know who you are as well. Luc. I'm not going to attempt your surname because I'll butcher it."

"It's Van den Bossche," he said.

I tried it and he laughed. "See?"

He shook his head. "I've heard worse."

I started wondering how old he was. He didn't look much younger than Brady. His skin was very tan, and he had a big build. Maybe just a little taller than Brady. A quieter charm to him.

"Have you been in Paris long?" I asked, wondering if he'd been to any of the shows.

"Only the last few days," he said.

"For fashion week?"

"Yes," he said. "I brought my sister. She always wanted to go."

"That's sweet of you."

He smiled. "I saw you walk in two shows."

"You did?"

"Yes, for Dior and Saint Laurent," he answered.

I was the only plus size model in both of those shows. Maybe that is why he remembered me.

"What did you think?" I asked, referring to the shows.

"I thought you were stunning."

I blushed a little and smiled. "I meant—"

He cut me off with a knowing smile. "I know what you meant."

He was handsome with hair a similar colour to Brady's. Blue eyes as well. But an interesting face rather than a beautiful one. Charming. A gorgeous accent. Beautiful hands. I wondered if he was single.

"Do you live in LA?"

"I don't. I don't have a house there. But I am there often. My agents would like me to make the move permanently."

"Of course."

"I'm heading there after this for a few weeks of press and then a shoot."

"Oh."

"I'll be there at least four months. Are you...? Are you heading home?"

"I am," I answered.

"Do you maybe want to get some dinner? When I'm in town."

There we go. "Yes. Sure."

"Let me get your phone number."

I took his phone and entered it in.

It had all gone terribly wrong when I gave Trevor Rhoda my phone number, but enough time had passed, I hoped, for things to go slightly better with Luc.

"I should be there on Sunday," he said. "I'll call you."

"Okay," I said, handing his phone back. "I should probably go back in. There are people I am supposed to meet."

"Good luck to you," he said.

There was that awkward moment then. Do we shake hands again? Hug? A pitiful wave? I didn't have to worry about it. Luc came closer, put a hand on my arm and kissed both of my cheeks. Very European.

"I'll see you soon," he said.

"See you soon," I answered. And, then he was walking away, quickly hidden in the dark of the Parisian streets. A very interesting possibility.

* * *

He did call. On the Sunday when he arrived in LA. "How about that dinner?" He asked, straight away.

"Really? You don't want to settle in?" I asked.

"I'm settled," he answered. "I want to take you to dinner."

He came to pick me up, in what I guessed was a rental, a black Escalade. He was dressed simply. A blue button down, blue jeans, grey coat, and brown dress shoes. I wore a light brown dress beneath my tan trench and chocolate brown ankle boots, so we matched in a very small way. He looked very handsome and very pleased to see me. He kissed both of my cheeks again in greeting.

"How are you?" I asked.

"I'm very well. I've been looking forward to this," he said.

"Me too," I answered honestly.

He drove us to a restaurant in Malibu. I tried to ignore the picture of Brady and I riding his Harley along the same roads that came up like a strobe in my mind. The restaurant was a formal place right on the cliffs. It had an incredible view of the ocean and the food, though portioned very small, was delicious.

Luc spoke of his work, the upcoming shoot, things he'd done in the past. I couldn't help but be reminded of Brady. I had done my research and Luc was 10 years younger than Brady. I wouldn't have known. He has a very mature look, I thought. Or maybe Brady just looks young for his age.

Luc showed a lot of interest in my own work and my history. I told him about my life back in New York and my friends and family back home in Alaska. He told me he loved to snowboard, and I told him there were incredible mountains in Alaska to do just that.

He was funny. I did laugh. Not nearly as much as I would've with Brady.

After dinner, he asked if I wanted to take a walk along the beach. Though it was cold, and I'd have to take my boots off, I agreed. One wave came crashing up, much further than the others, soaking our feet.

"Oh my god," I screamed. "That's freezing."

At some point, the cold became too much, and we ran back to the car.

"The sand," I said, looking down at my feet.

"It's fine," he insisted.

We climbed into the car and turned up the heat, warming ourselves up.

"Home then?" He asked when we were fully warm.

We drove the winding roads back to my new place and Luc walked me to my door.

"I had a really nice time," I said, sincerely.

"Me too," he said with a smile.

I opened my door and looked back at him. He leaned in and kissed my cheek. One then the other. And, then he kissed my lips. I held my boots in my hands in front of me, blocking him from coming too close or from me touching him, but his hands came up to my cheeks, holding me as he kissed me gently, deepening the kiss just a little, touching my tongue with his. Finally, needing a breath, he pulled away, but only a little.

I dropped my shoes as I threw my hands over his shoulders. I brought his mouth back to mine, stroking his tongue as I stroked his short hair with my fingers. I imagined his thin lips fuller, like Brady's. Fucking hell. I was doing it again.

"Can I come inside?" He asked, quietly, when we broke away again.

I swallowed. I'd done this to Trevor. That was beyond fucked up. Luc pulled away a little more.

"We don't have to do anything," he said. "Just talk. Just this." He kissed me again, a little deeper. It was a good kiss. I'm sure the rest of it would've been good too, but all I'd be thinking about would be Brady. I pulled away a little myself and shook my head.

"Not tonight," I said.

"No?" He asked, that same small smile.

"No," I said.

He nodded. "Okay."

He started walking away, not annoyed, just resigned.

"I'm sorry," I said, that annoying part of me not wanting to displease anyone.

He turned back to look at me with a smile. "For what?" So casual. He smiled again, gave something of a nod, then got into his car and drove away.

Because the whole time, I was thinking of Brady.

I'd said I'd loved him. I'd thought it long before that. It was the first time I'd ever felt that way. The first time I'd said it to a man. I knew we hadn't been even dating. Not boyfriend and girlfriend. We'd never given ourselves a label but the closest thing to what we were was a kind of friends with benefits. Yet, I'd fallen for him. Stupidly.

I thought it would be hard to get over him. But hard as I imagined it, I thought I could do it. In time. People got over their first loves. But it wasn't happening for me. Not with time. Not with dating. No amount of work or distraction could keep my mind from wandering to him. It scared me.

A week or so later, Odessa told me she'd booked another gig to shoot after her Richard Rodriguez project. She was raking in the cash now, and though I'd been able to afford a place on my own for a while, she was finally ready to move out, too. As much as we'd loved living together, if we could afford to have our own places, the privacy of your own home was undeniable. We decided to look in the same area. We didn't want to separate too far.

We both found places in the Beverly Hills area and helped each other make the move. It was a hard adjustment but when we timed it out, we were still only 6 minutes from each other. That would work. Though I guessed Odessa wouldn't be staying there long. She and Eti were growing ever more serious.

His birthday came and he flew her to New York to meet his friends and family. After that we all went down to Mexico for a weekend of drinking and beaching. Though I'd been avoiding my phone, my attention was drawn to an article about fighting on set between Brady and Theo. That didn't seem like him at all. I knew how professional he was.

Days after that, after we'd all returned home, there were pictures everywhere of an argument between Brady and Catalina. They were outside a lawyer's office and screaming at each other.

I wanted so badly to reach out and make sure he was okay. I tried to convince myself I could. That just because we weren't dating anymore, didn't mean I couldn't be a friend to him. But I couldn't bring myself to do it. I was too cowardly. I thought it would hurt. The same reason I refused to go the Oscars with Odessa. She'd been invited. I had to say no. She was disappointed, but she understood. She must've thought I was an idiot for getting myself so into Brady when he obviously never had any intention for us beyond the secretive casual nature of what we had. I thought I was an idiot, too.

* * *

The TV was there and off, a black screen, my own reflection staring back at me. The two warring sides of me played out the conversation of whether to turn it on and switch to the right channel.

I wanted to see Odessa at the Oscars. I didn't want to see Brady. You always watch the Oscars, I told myself. Are you gonna change that this year for some guy? Not just some guy.

A knock on the door brought me back to reality. It guessed it was the

Uber Eats I'd ordered. I fixed my hair a little for the stranger. There was nothing I could do about the old pajamas.

I swung open the door with a casual smile. My mouth dropped. My eyes widened. My breathing stopped altogether. It wasn't Uber Eats. In front of me, in a black tuxedo, stood Brady fucking Witter.

CHAPTER THIRTEEN:

Loving him was RED

BRADY

She wasn't supposed to love me. There were supposed to be no feelings. Just sex. Just fun. She was a rebound. After a decade of marriage. Sure, I'd come to care for her more than I'd meant to. She was too sweet, too beautiful, and we seemed to fit so well together, I couldn't help it. But I didn't love her. She wasn't supposed to fall for me.

I felt like the worst piece of shit watching her walk away from me. I felt guilty because I was the one who pushed it. I'd sought her out. She was happily going along ignoring me. If I hadn't chased after her, twice, then none of this would've happened, I told myself.

Well, it was done then. I walked out of the lobby, into the night, where everyone was trying to get into their cars and to the after parties. I was grabbed by an old friend, another actor, Mark. He looked concerned.

"I heard you got into a fight with some girl?" He said. "Is everything okay?

"Oh yeah. It was nothing. Are people..." I started to get worried. "What are people saying?"

"It just looked like you were fighting, and she was upset. Who was she?"

"Just a girl."

"Someone you're dating?" He asked. Too many questions.

"No," I answered.

He nodded. I wasn't sure he believed me. He as well as some other of my friends were heading to the after party. I couldn't do that. Especially if people were curious about Haven and me. I didn't want to be fielding questions. I headed home.

∗ ∗ ∗

Before we'd met, I'd never seen her before in my life. Suddenly she was popping up all over the place. There were pictures of her walking the runways in Milan.

She was a guest on my favorite podcast. I had skipped her episode, but I went back to it. A glutton for punishment. She was just as charming on there as she always was in person. Completely herself. She didn't talk about me, why would she? She talked about the industry, going into plus size modeling and some of the glass ceilings that hadn't yet been knocked down that she had smashed through. The host asked her about her dating life and mentioned that she'd been rumored to be dating Trevor Rhoda. Another rumored love interest was Luc Van den Bossche. I knew both of them. Great actors. Good looking guys. I hated them.

I even saw her just walking down the street in Beverly Hills. If there was a god, he seemed to be torturing me.

At night, instead of going out and meeting a girl my age, someone I could possibly have a future with, I thought about Haven. I thought about the way we danced that first night. I thought about how expressive her blue eyes were. I thought about how her long dark hair always smelled good, felt soft in my hands, dusted the top of her bare back when she got out of bed in the morning.

The day after the film wrapped, I had a meeting with Catalina and our lawyers. She was dragging this thing out and I was over it.

I walked into the office and found her waiting with her lawyer, a tall thin serious looking man, in the lobby. I told the receptionist who I was and who I was waiting for and she called my lawyer. I went to sit by Cat, kissing her cheek and introducing myself to her lawyer. She stayed silent as we waited. The short bespectacled woman who'd been my lawyer for decades came out shortly after.

"Good morning," she said, reaching out to shake Cat's hand. They knew each other.

The lawyers introduced themselves to each other and we all walked into the conference room.

They began going through the simple things, the things we'd already agreed to. She was keeping the house we'd shared. She was keeping the Escalade, the Bentley she wanted, and the house we'd bought for her mother in Mexico. Then we came to the more difficult things. She wanted the house and winery in Tuscany, that I'd bought before we'd married. She wanted a share of the film and the bike businesses. She wanted a million dollars per year per kid 'til they were eighteen. I was happy to give the kids everything they needed and more, but she was kidding herself. Especially since she earned nearly as much as me. And, the last and worst of all her demands was that I only be guaranteed visits every second week and not at all if it didn't suit her schedule.

We started with the easiest. In exchange for her dropping any claim to my businesses, I gave up the villa. Time would tell what was worth more, but there were other villas. I was glad I had been there one last time, and with Haven.

We haggled on the child support with Alice reminding Cat what she earned in the last five years of our marriage. But the kids would be living with Cat. We got the amount down to $1.5 million per year total. She reluctantly agreed.

And then there was the final matter and as well as the negotiations had gone until then, in comparison to how they'd gone every previous occasion, they slowed to a full stop.

"My client is involved with incredibly important work on behalf of the United Nations and absolutely refuses to negotiate on those points."

"Her UN trips are once a year if that. If I miss a visit for that, I don't mind. But it isn't fair that I don't get to see my kids every time she has a shoot."

"Brady." Alice touched my arm to quiet me. She started arguing on my behalf. Cat sat there taking it for barely five minutes before standing up.

"I don't have to listen to this. I'm done."

"Cat," her lawyer plead but she was gone. I got up and chased after her, finding her on the street searching for her car keys.

"What are you doing?"

"What are you doing letting your lawyer attack me like that?" she screamed.

"She wasn't attacking you, she was making reasonable points," I answered, trying to calm her. "With this agreement, you'd have every right to keep me from my kids indefinitely."

"As if I would do that," Cat threw up her hands.

"I can't be sure of that," I answered quietly.

She huffed. "That's what you think of me? I'm some evil hag trying to keep you from your children?"

"Of course not," I answered. "But I never thought you'd just kick me out either. Without giving me the chance to fix things."

"You had plenty of chances."

"And, what about Mannix? Why don't you care that I haven't seen my son in months?"

"I don't control him."

"Have you talked to him? He needs a father."

Cat found her keys, unlocked her car and threw her bag in the passenger seat.

"Where are you going?" I asked. "We're not finished."

"Yes, we are. Sign the papers or don't."

She walked around to the driver's side and I chased after her. "Please don't do this, Cat. I can't give up everything."

"What have you given up? Nothing. Not really. I have no rights to the businesses I helped build." She had to be kidding me. She was in one film I produced and had never been near the bike business.

"My villa?"

"You spent your days there getting drunk and high, you were barely there. What else? That girl?"

"What?" I snapped back, furious.

"That kid you were fucking; do you count her? Was that a sacrifice you made?"

"I don't want to fight about this. I just want to have the right to see my kids as much as I can."

"You can!" she screamed.

"When it's convenient for you!" I met her volume. "That's bullshit!"

I heard the clicking at the same time she did. We were being photographed.

I lowered my voice. "How did it come to this?"

Cat stilled. The expression on her face softened. It reminded me of the Cat I fell in love with. "I don't know."

I opened my mouth, but I didn't know how to respond to that. She got in the car and drove away. I didn't blame her. I didn't want the kids to see us in some magazine screaming at each other outside a lawyer's office.

I don't know, she'd said. She had been the one driving this thing. I hadn't been able to understand any of it, but I thought she must've known how she was feeling. But maybe she didn't know either.

Either way, whether we had been truly in love or not, neither of us felt that way anymore. I realized then that there might never be any explanation. And I would have to make my peace with that.

* * *

I had another few weeks with nothing to do. I might have flown to Tuscany if I still owned the place. I might have rode down to Mexico. All I had was my little Hollywood Hills place. And, it felt too small. Haven had bought every comforting thing in there. I thought I should throw it all out and start from scratch, but I couldn't bring myself to take any of those steps.

One afternoon, after a long ride nowhere in particular, Charlie, the leggy red headed supermodel turned actress who'd accosted me at the Golden Globes, sent me a text.

Charlie: *Hey, it's Charlie.*

Brady: *Hey. How are you?*

Charlie: *I'm good. Ready for you to take me out?*

Brady: *Did we make a plan?*

Charlie: *I made a plan haha*

Did I like her? I barely knew her. She was beautiful, in her own way. What else did I have to do?

Brady: *Okay. You free right now?*

She was. I got myself ready and drove out to pick her up. She didn't live too far from me in the Hills. I walked to her door and knocked. She opened it, holding her top to her body. "Hey! Can you help me with this?"

She turned around, her bare back on display. "Sure," I answered as I zipped up the top. It seemed like something she could've done on her own.

"Give me two minutes?"

I nodded. I stepped carefully into her living room, trying to hide my distaste at the mess it was in. Her coffee table was littered with scripts and magazines and old takeaway containers. A massive dog bed covered in fur was set beside the couch, its pungent scent filling the room.

"Okay," Charlie said, coming back into the room with a purse in hand. "Ready?"

I nodded and led her out to my car.

"A Tesla?" she asked, surprised. "Humble."

"Under the radar," I answered.

She nodded. "Got it."

We drove to a small Italian restaurant in Los Feliz and were given a somewhat private table toward the back.

"I've never been here before," she said as I pushed in her chair. "It's charming."

The curl of her lip made me think she thought it was anything but. We ordered a couple of pizzas and a salad, and a bottle of red wine. I was going to need it if I had to listen to more of her stories. She was in the midst of a story about how a director insisted that anyone who wanted to be on set for the shooting of a sex scene in her recent film, had to likewise be naked.

"I didn't ask him to do that. I was fine. Cause honestly, I don't really have a problem being naked."

I nodded, making a mental note not to work with a director who insisted on his crew being naked.

"Does that sound slutty?" she asked.

"A little," I joked.

She flirtingly hit me on the shoulder. "Shut the fuck up!"

"And anyway, I'd been working out like crazy to lose the weight from my last gig."

"I've seen that trailer. Looks like an incredible performance."

"Thank you," she smiled cheesily.

"But, I am never putting weight on for a role again. It's just a nightmare losing it all. I was in the gym for at least two hours a day."

I nodded, feigning interest.

"But that is probably your everyday routine? I mean you look incredible."

"Not really," I answered. An hour a day is my limit.

"You're so full of shit," she fawned. "Your body is insane. What do you do?"

"I just try and stay active," I answered.

"Yeah? I love a bit of rock-climbing, you know? Riding out to the desert and finding a good boulder…"

None of what she was saying felt authentic. It felt like she was saying what she thought I wanted to hear. She was just trying so hard to be cool.

We finished our meal and I excused myself to go to the bathroom and then pay the check.

"You ready?" I asked.

"Yeah? Are we paid?"

"I got it," I answered.

"Wow. Gentleman. Doesn't mean you're getting laid," she insisted.

I didn't even know how to respond to that one. I drove her home and walked her to the door. She turned back to look at me expectantly. I leaned in and kissed her cheek. "Nice to see you," I said before turning around.

She came after me, grabbing my shoulders and turning me around. "I was kidding about you not getting laid," she said as she grabbed my neck and started kissing me, too deeply, too quickly. I shifted back a little. "Let's go inside?"

I took her hand off my neck. "I've got an early morning."

"Seriously?" she asked, disappointment lining her face.

"Seriously," I answered. "Thanks for tonight."

She threw her hands up in the air. "Yeah, okay."

I got back into my car and drove off. What a waste of a night.

As I drove home, I took the long way. I visited those places I'd looked for Mannix when he'd gone missing. The places he'd go to skate, the friends' houses I used to take him to, hoping against hope that I might run into him. I couldn't find him anywhere. I was about to go home when I changed my mind. I drove to my old house. You couldn't see much from the other side of the fence, but I imagined that it looked exactly the same inside. It was almost 10pm. The girls would be in bed. Mannix and Cat would still be awake.

As I was considering braving Cat's wrath to go inside and talk to my son, he rode up on a push bike, and started to take his key out of his backpack. Without thinking, I got out of my car and rushed over.

As he heard my steps, he turned around. "It's me," I said, realizing he probably couldn't see me in the dark.

"What are you doing here?" I hadn't spoken to him in months and that was the first thing he said?

"I came to see you," I answered. "You haven't been answering my calls."

"So maybe take a hint."

He found his key and opened the gate. I reached over and grabbed it keeping it closed.

"I'm your dad, Mannix. Let me talk to you for a second."

He pushed against the gate. "Get out of my way!"

I reached out and touched his arm, tormented by all this anger he seemed to have toward me. "Why are you so angry?"

"Why the fuck do you think?" He'd never sworn at me before.

"I'm sorry. I'm sorry about your mother and me." She didn't give me a chance to talk to the kids when it ended. She wanted to tell them herself. It was the first time I started to question exactly what she told them.

"Yeah, don't act like you give a shit now when you just left. Get your hand off the door!" He hit out at me.

"What did you say?" I asked, letting it go. "That I left?"

He started to push his bike into the yard, and I followed.

"You're not supposed to be in here," he said, his voice getting quieter. He was getting upset. I didn't want to push him, but I needed to know what he thought.

"I didn't just leave. She made me go. I never would have left you guys. No matter how bad things might've been between us. I would have tried everything."

He stopped walking and turned back toward me.

"I swear, Mannix. It's the truth."

"She told me you walked out."

I almost laughed. "Are you serious?"

Mannix nodded, confused, a little nervous.

182

The door opened, flooding light over us and Cat appeared on the deck. "What are you doing here?" she demanded angrily, as if she had any right.

"You told the kids I left you?" I asked, trying to keep calm.

Cat realized what I knew and raised her chin, unwilling to accept any blame at all.

"How could you say that to them? How the fuck could you do that?" I yelled, taking a step back.

"Don't yell at her!" Mannix said, as Cat answered. "You'll wake up the kids."

"I'm sorry," I said to Mannix. And, taking my chance; "I love you."

I turned around and walked out.

I kept fuming all night. I woke up furious. I called Catalina but she didn't answer. I called her again and again, all day long until she did. She was ready for a fight. I demanded she tell the kids what really happened.

"To me, you did leave. Long before I asked you to."

"Whatever you need to tell yourself. You tell the kids the truth."

"Mannix knows the truth. I only told the girls that we broke up. Not that you left me."

I barely believed her. I'd talk to the girls on my own, the next time I saw them. It killed me to think that they thought I walked out on them. I hated to know that Mannix had been walking around for months thinking that was what happened.

I sent Mannix a text, asking him to come visit me with his sisters. He finally responded. It was only to tell me that he was busy, but it was at the very least a start. I texted him again a couple days later, just to ask how he was doing. He answered again, that he was good, that he was looking to buy a new push bike. It made me smile. It sounded like he wanted some cash. But that meant that we could do something together. I'd take it.

* * *

"This one?" I asked. It was the most basic bike. Matte black all over, low riding, nothing special.

"Yep," Mannix answered, characteristically monosyllabic.

"Okay," I said, nodding at the store clerk.

"Great. Anything else today?" He knew who I was. He was hoping for a nice commission. I looked to Mannix. He shook his head. I looked to the girls who seemed to be uninterested in the whole activity.

"I think we're okay," I answered. The clerk looked disappointed. The bike was half a grand, I thought. He would have a fine commission. The bike was a little pricey, but I would've spent a lot more for Mannix to spend a little time with me. I'd even managed to convince him to go to lunch with me and the girls.

I paid for the bike and we got it easily into the trunk of the car. "So, lunch?"

"Yes, I'm hungry!" Vera said.

"What do we feel like?" I looked at each of my kids, heart swelling at the thought of being able to spend the day with them all.

"Burgers?" Zola suggested. "Or Chinese food?"

I looked to Mannix. He shrugged. "No requests?"

He pursed his lips a little. "We could get something and take it down to the park."

"Yeah? Girls?"

"Burgers?" Zola repeated.

I looked to Vera. "You want a burger?"

"Okay," she answered.

We pulled out of the carpark and went to find ourselves a few burgers and a whole bunch of chips to take down to the park.

I knew which park he meant. He wanted to try out the new bike.

We got the bike back out and Mannix took off straight away.

"What about your lunch?"

"I'll come back for it!" Mannix shouted behind him as he rode toward the ramps.

The girls and I found a spot to picnic, away from others but near enough to the ramps to watch Mannix.

My phone vibrated as I finished the last of my burger.

Catalina: *Where are you?*

I answered. *At the skate park.*

She fired back straight away. *I'm at your house.*

I huffed a little. She was half an hour early. *We'll be home soon*, I answered.

The girls continued eating and Mannix continued to skate, forgetting all about his burger. I took the girls over to the swings. Zola wasn't too excited by them, but Vera hadn't got over the novelty yet. I pushed them both on the swings but kept an eye on Mannix.

I watched as he positioned himself at the top of a vert ramp. He seemed to be gearing up for something. I stopped the girls on the swings. "I think your brother is going to do a trick," I told them.

Zola hopped off.

"I can't see," Vera said. I lifted her into my arms. We watched together as Mannix pushed off and rode down the ramp and up the other side, turned, and went back. He rode back and forth. The girls and I wandered over, still watching, until finally he flew into the air bringing himself upside down and making a 180 degree turn.

Zola and Vera gasped.

"Holy shit!" I said, not quietly enough.

Mannix came out of the ramp and dumped his bike, elated. A few of the other riders, none of them his actual friends, gave him some props but when he saw us standing there and rushed over.

"Did you see it?" He asked.

"I saw it," I answered, just as enthusiastically.

"It was a flair."

"It was awesome," I said, giving him a squeeze on the shoulder.

"Good job, Mannix," Zola said, holding up her hand for a high five. Mannix gave it enthusiastically, to Zola then Vera and finally me.

I heard a quiet clap and turned to see Catalina walking over.

"Mom, did you see it?"

"I saw it, baby! So good," she said.

"I'm going to try again," Mannix said, started off back to his bike. Zola rushed to her mother and I dropped Vera down to do the same. Catalina leaned down and hugged them both tightly.

"Did you have a good day?" she asked.

"Really good," Zola answered.

"Hi," I said, as Catalina arrived at my side.

"Hi," she answered.

"I'm sorry. I was going to leave about now to get home on time," I assured her.

"It's fine," she said, in a tone I hadn't heard from her in a very long time.

I turned to notice the look in her eyes. "What?" I asked.

"Nothing," she answered, quickly. "We should get going."

I nodded. "Mannix," I called out. He pulled up on the ramp and nodded, understanding.

I walked with them all back to Catalina's car. I said goodbye to the girls as they got into the car, giving them good squeezes and telling them I loved them. Mannix rode over and I helped him put the bike into the car.

"Thanks for the bike, Dad," he said, as we shut the trunk.

"You're welcome," I said. He looked at me as if considering whether to hug me. I wasn't going to force it, but I was thankful when he wrapped his arms around me of his own accord.

"Love you," I said, as he pulled away. I definitely didn't expect to hear that back from him. "I'll see you soon."

"Okay," He answered, and walked around to the passenger side. I walked toward Catalina who stood by her closed driver door.

"Thanks for coming to get them," I said, though I hadn't asked her to.

She nodded. I stood there awkwardly a moment, wondering whether or not to reach and open her door, when she spoke. "You're a good dad."

My mouth dropped open in surprise.

She reached over and pushed my chin up, closing my mouth for me. She opened the car door and got in. I took a few steps back, still speechless, and waved to the kids as she drove away.

✳ ✳ ✳

On the day of the Oscars, another event that I'd attend alone, my mind started playing out the scenarios as I dressed into another black tux. I seemed to have no control over it.

I imagined the possibility of the few photos we took together being leaked to the public. I imagined the uproar about Haven's age. People would be saying the thing I had thought so early on. That she was barely older than Mannix. It was so soon after Catalina, I must have cheated. They'd say she was using me. Maybe they'd think she wanted to be an actress. They'd think I was having a mid-life crisis. But it would be done. It would be out there. And, then we'd just deal with whatever shit was thrown our way, together. Including whatever Cat decided to do. Since that day at the park and those four words, I couldn't imagine her ever keeping me from my kids. No matter how much she wanted to punish me. She'd give me a hard time, I didn't doubt that. But then, maybe, it would all die down. We'd stay together for the rest of our lives and then people couldn't say shit because we were meant to be.

If I won the Oscar, I could thank her in my speech. If I were genuine enough, if I told her I loved her, then and there in front of millions of people, maybe the world would be more forgiving.

Love her? I didn't mean that.

Anyway, she'd have to forgive me first. I obviously hurt her. I didn't mean to, but I did. She was still too young for me. Too good for me. Maybe that is what I'd always meant by those words. Not too young but too good. I was older, but it wasn't even about the age. I'd lived so much of life already. I'd made a lot of terrible choices and had a ton of baggage including three kids and a pissed off ex. She didn't deserve to be weighed down with that. I loved her too much to put that on her.

I love her. It's not just slips of the tongue or the mind. I do, I thought. I have for a long time. I thought Gwendolyn was the one, but she didn't even come close. Then I thought it was supposed to be Cat all along. That we were supposed to marry and have kids and become a family. But with Haven, nothing felt right on paper. It shouldn't have worked but it did. It felt more right when we were kissing, talking, holding each other, than anything ever had.

I love her, I thought. But it didn't change a thing. Unless I could be brave. I wasn't a kid. I needed to stop being such a fucking coward. I loved her. And, if she still loved me then we should be together. And, fuck anyone who has anything to say about it.

I could've called her and asked her to meet but I had somewhere to be and I wanted her to be there with me. I called Odessa instead.

"Brady?" She asked questioningly. I could hear bustling in the background. I guessed her hair and makeup team. She was attending the same event. I wondered if Haven was in the room with her.

"Is Haven there?" I asked.

"What?"

"Haven, is she there?" I asked again.

"No. She... we got our own places." She sounded confused.

"Oh," I swallowed. "Can you give me her new address? Do you know if she'll be there?"

"What's this about?" She asked, sounding defensive now.

"I've been a fucking idiot," I said.

I heard Odessa scoff out a laugh. "Yeah," she said finally. "You have."

"I need to see her," I said, taking out a paper and pen in the hope that she'd tell me what I needed to know.

She started telling me the address and I wrote it all down. "She's home."

"Thank you," I said.

"Don't hurt her again," Odessa said, insistent.

"I'll do my best," I said, ready to hang up.

"Do better than that," she demanded.

"I will," I answered. "Bye."

My town car arrived, the one taking me to the show, and I gave him the new first stop.

We reached the house. A bungalow in Beverly Hills with a yellow-colored exterior and a red tiled roof. There were rows of flowers beneath the windows and a big plant beside her door over which you found the doorbell. I pressed it and held my breath.

The door flew open, like she had been waiting for someone. But then she realized it was me and her mouth dropped. She looked so cute, in her pink pajamas, her hair piled high on her head.

"Hi," I said, releasing my breath and smiling at her.

Her brows furrowed. She crossed her arms over herself, obviously a little embarrassed to be caught in that state. I wanted to tell her she was adorable.

"What are you doing here?" She asked. "Aren't you supposed to be at the Oscars?"

"I am. I wanted to see if you'd go with me."

"What?"

"I wanted to see if you'd be my date to the Oscars," I asked.

She shook her head, looking over my shoulder to the town car parked on the street. "I'm confused."

"I changed my mind. I don't give a shit what anyone thinks. I mean, I do. You know that. But I care about you more." I felt so certain of this now.

I watched her swallow. She shook her head a little trying to wrap her head around it. "Since when?"

"Honestly... a couple of hours ago."

She huffed. "So, you've just decided this. After weeks since... months since we've been together. You decide today?"

"I know," I said. I couldn't expect her to feel the same certainty. "I've been an idiot. I've been trying to convince myself that it isn't right but it's like you said... it's useless."

"You're just over the age thing?" She asked.

"Not over it. I'm just going to deal with it," I said.

"What about Catalina?"

I took a breath. "It'll be okay. We'll deal with it."

"We'll deal with it?" She repeated.

I nodded as assuredly as I could.

"I don't believe it."

"So, come with me? Let everyone see." I started to fear that it wasn't going to be as easy as I'd hoped. Maybe I'd hurt her beyond what I'd thought.

"What makes you think I didn't take your advice? Carter could be in this house right now," she teased.

I couldn't laugh. "Is he? Did you?"

She shook her head. She grew serious.

"You really hurt me," she said. "I've been hurting all this time."

"I'm sorry," I said, honestly. I hated the thought of her in pain and pain of my doing.

"But... what if you regret it?" She seemed terrified.

"I don't know. I can't tell you I won't. But I already regret losing you.

And, it can't feel worse than that."

"I'm scared," she said, wrapping her arms around herself a little tighter.

I hated that she was scared. That it was hard to believe me. I needed to convince her. "I know I've screwed you around. I know that. But you said you loved me. And, I can't stop thinking about it. I used to dream about fucking you. Now all I want to do is love you."

She looked back up at me. The last two words hitting her. "Love me?" She asked quietly.

"I love you, Haven Roser."

"You do?" Her arms dropped back to her sides.

"I do," I said, earnestly. "Do you maybe still love me?"

She smiled, bitting her lip through it. "Maybe." Tease.

"You haven't fallen in love with some Belgian?"

"Who told you about that?" She asked, shocked. "Odessa?"

"Not Odessa. She did give me your address though. I like the new place."

"Thank you."

"So how about it?" He asked.

"What was the question again?" She asked, smiling.

"Do you love me? Will you go to the Oscars with me so I can tell everyone who's watching that you're mine?"

"I don't have a dress..." she said, deflating.

"I know you have dresses..." I said, I'd seen them on her.

"Not for the Oscars..." she said, starting to stress.

"It doesn't have to be a ball gown," I said.

"Wait!" She jumped a little. "I have something."

She turned around and rushed up the stairs. She reached the fifth step and then jumped back down, rushing across the doorway and into my arms. She crushed a kiss against my lips, wrapped her arms around my neck, her legs around my waist. The kiss answered that first question. She still loved me. And, I was the luckiest man alive.

She jumped off then and ran back up the stairs. "It was an alternate from the Globes. Give me five minutes."

She was down in seven minutes, showered, in a red lace dress, her hair styled into a loose bun, black heels, jewels, the whole thing. "What do you think?" She asked.

"You're incredible."

We rushed toward the town car, knowing we'd be late. I spent the fifteen-minute drive going back and forth between making out with her and holding up a mirror so she could do her make up.

When we arrived in the line, there were only a couple of cars ahead of us. She kissed me one last time before putting on a pink lipstick.

"You ready?" I asked, reaching for the door. She grabbed my hand.

"Are you? We don't have to do this," she said, giving me an out.

I didn't need one. I'd found my courage and more than that, I wanted her there with me.

I opened the door. Quickly they were screaming my name. I held a hand out for Haven and she took it, stepping gracefully out of the car. The voices came quickly.

"Oh my god!"

"That's Haven Roser."

"Are they together?"

"BRADY! HAVEN!"

I kept Haven's hand in mine. She was shaking a little.

"Are you okay?" I asked her. I never thought about the fact that she'd be scared. But of course, it was changing her life, too.

"Yes," she said. "I love you."

"I love you, too."

I leaned in and kissed her cheek.

The crowd erupted. The photographers, the fans, the media line. They were going nuts.

"Let's go," I said, pulling her along with me, her hand in mine. We declined all invitations to interview, whether for me specifically or Haven. We did however stand in front of the photographers. I put an arm around Haven and she occasionally looked up and me. We let them scream and ask their questions, we gave no response. Until one of them yelled out, "how about a kiss?"

Haven looked up at me with a smile. "How about it?" I asked her.

She bit her lip and smiled. I put both arms around her, catching her by surprise, dipping her back like the nurse and sailor on VJ Day. The screaming increased by what sounded like a thousandfold.

I lifted her back up and she opened her eyes, laughing. My heart soared to see her so happy.

We did win the Oscar. And, I did thank her. "My love, Haven."

HAVEN

Did I give in too easily? Who fucking cares! This is the thing I'd been praying for. I was never getting over him. I knew that. Was I terrified he'd hurt me again? Yes. But no matter what anyone ever did, I couldn't tear my heart from my sleeve. I couldn't tear it from him. He would have it forever. So, I gave in. And, he declared to all the world that I was his.

"I still can't believe it," I said, as his car took us to the after party.

"Believe it," Brady said, taking my hand and planting a kiss there.

We arrived at the venue, the Ellis Shannon Centre of Performing Arts, and walked down another red carpet, stopping for pictures in front of the huge 'VANITY FAIR' sign. We skipped the interviewers again and made our way inside.

The party itself was held in a massive entertaining room. There was a stage with a DJ playing music for the movie stars dancing on the dancefloor. In opposite corners of the room were bars, four people deep and between them tables seating a dozen guests. As we walked into the room, all eyes turned to us - there was something about Brady - and he started introducing me to the people who approached. As "my girlfriend, Haven." It was overwhelming, but I couldn't have been happier. It all felt so surreal.

Eti and Odessa found us soon after, and we all went to the bar for drinks. It felt a little odd, the four of us, but Eti was a great admirer of Brady's and they seemed to get on surprisingly well. So much so, that Odessa and I left them to chat and mind our drinks as we went off dancing. "I'm so happy," I said to Odessa as she brought me close.

"I'm so happy for you!" she said. "But if he hurts you again, I'll kill him."

We cackled.

I looked back over at Brady and Eti who had been quickly surrounded by a group of men. Brady was captivating them with a story. His smile was so magnetic, I could feel it from across the room. I wanted to kiss him. I wanted to do more than that.

Odessa leaned into me again. "Go get him."

I looked back at her and she nodded, gesturing for me to go back to him. I smiled and ran off the dancefloor, rushing over to Brady. I took a step in between two of the men and caught Brady's attention. He smiled at me.

"Can I steal him away?" I asked.

"You sure can," the man to my right said, along with a few other muttered agreements. Brady stepped out of their circle and I grabbed his hand. I led him out of the room, out to the foyer where a security guard was talking to a drunk guest.

"Is that Ryan?" Brady asked quietly as I stopped him by the stairs. "What are we doing?" he asked.

I smiled. As the security guard at the other end of the room turned around, I pulled Brady again and started up the stairs. Brady caught on quickly, rushing up ahead of me and pulling me around the corner and out of sight.

I'd been to the building before. I knew there was an upper level encircling the hall below with shelves of books running off the railing like a library. It was all dark and out of bounds, but we'd gotten there. Brady and I walked quietly around, looking down the darkened hallways and offices off the main path. We were alone up there. I pulled him between one of the lots of shelves, toward the railing. We looked down at the party still raging. Brady stood behind me, his arms around me. He pressed a kiss to my shoulder. "Here?" he asked.

"I want you," I answered. I'd been wanting him.

"I want you," he answered, running his hands up my thighs and around my waist. "I've been dying to touch you again."

"Have you?" I asked. I couldn't imagine him wanting me half as much as I wanted him. His hands came up to cup my breasts and already I was shivering. "Show me," I pleaded, grinding my ass into his crotch.

He groaned a little, still massaging my breasts in his hands. I reached down and lifted my dress as far as it could go. Brady's hands went to my bare ass. "Fuck," he said, as he rounded my hips and found my already wet cunt. He felt the flesh there, running his fingers along the wetness, spreading it around and finding my bundle of nerves. I threw my head back against his chest as he explored, folding forward as he bent over delving two fingers into me. I cried out a little and he shushed me.

"Did Luc Van den Bossche make you feel like this?" There was that jealousy.

He took his fingers away from me and I whined. "Brady…"

"Did he?"

"No!" I said, a little too loudly. I closed my mouth as his fingers returned and heard Brady's quiet laughter in my ear.

Brady added another finger, stretching me out like the god he was, and I fell forward with the pleasure. Brady leaned forward too, lifting my back up and holding me against him as he pumped his fingers in and out of me.

"Did he fuck you?"

"No," I said.

"No?" he repeated.

"No!" I answered. "We barely kissed."

He shushed me with a laugh. "You have to stay quiet."

"No. You have to fuck me," I said quietly. I reached back to feel his hard cock and he let go of me to undo his pants. I turned to help him, but he already had it out and was forcefully turning me back around. The force turned me on, I ground my bare ass into him again. He lined me up and pressed the tip of his cock to my entrance.

"Did Trevor?"

"What?" I said, exasperated, my voice trembling.

"Did Trevor fuck you?"

I was suddenly terrified. Had I ruined everything? On a couple of stupid thrusts?

I turned my head just a little and looked at Brady. I didn't have to say it.

"I'm sorry," I said. "Please don't be mad."

"You have no reason to be sorry," he said, quietly. "I'm just going to have to make you forget about him."

I wanted to tell him that Trevor had been inside me for about five seconds. And, that entire time I'd been thinking of Brady. But the masochistic part of me loved the jealousy, loved that he felt just a little bit bigger and harder at my entrance when he knew. I'd tell him the truth of it later. I ground back into him again and he ran the head of his dick up and down my wet folds.

"Don't scream," he said. I bent over a little, resting my head on my arm on the railing, biting into my flesh just as he pressed into me. The sensation was unbearably good. He couldn't contain his own mumbled. "Fuck."

He pulled out a little and pushed back in. I cried out a little. He shushed me again as he ran a palm up my back, over my neck and into my hair before turning my head and bringing my lips back to him. My mouth opened as I cried out as he thrust into me again. God, I'd missed his perfect cock and how fucking incredible it made me feel. He ran his other hand up my stomach and kneaded at my breast as he held my head in the crook of his elbow, his hand coming to cover my mouth as I kept steady at the railing.

I felt that torturous coiling at my core as he started to pound into me. My clit pulsed desperate to be touched and his fingers found me immediately. He let go of my head as he held my hip with one hand, slamming into my cunt as he rubbed at my clit with the other. The song suddenly changed, a loud bop that allowed me to let out a scream as my orgasm took over me. I felt Brady's cock grow in me, clenched in the walls of my pussy as I came around him, bringing on his own orgasm. He shot into me as his head fell on my back, his head a little wet with sweat. I rode his cock as I rode my orgasm, as we both came down.

When we were ready, he pulled out of me and did up his pants. I was still leaning on the railing when he pulled me away. He held me up against the set of shelves, straightening my dress, bringing it back down my thighs and brushing the hair away from my face.

"I love you," he said, a little breathlessly.

"I love you," I answered, leaning forward in my exhaustion and kissing his soft lips. He tipped my chin up a little as he opened my mouth and touched my tongue, tenderly. He took my top lip in his, then my bottom, kissing me as lovingly as he ever had. We kissed like that for a few moments and then made our way back downstairs.

We got one look, from the security guard still dealing with the drunkard, but he shrugged it off. We didn't go back into the party. We went home. We had more loving to do.

We arrived back at his place just before 1am. Brady locked the door behind him and then helped me off with my shoes, then my dress. He laid me down on his big comfortable bed and then stripped down himself. I might've fallen asleep if the view wasn't so damn good. The Adonis in front of me was mine, I thought. Those pale blue eyes, that big sharp jaw, those full lips and perfect teeth, his lean rippling muscles, his long thick cock and all of it mine.

"What are you looking at?" he asked. I didn't know how long I'd been laying there staring at him. I just smiled.

He took a step closer, putting a knee onto the bed and bending down to press a kiss to each of my feet. He ran his hands, his lips, up my legs until he came to my mound. He pressed a kiss there and then spread my legs, opening me up to him. He brought his mouth back to me and licked and sucked at me until I was soaking again for him. I reached to his neck, bringing him up to lay beside me. I kissed his lips and then made a trail down his neck, his body, to his cock, taking him into my mouth, getting him hard and ready for me again, before he was pulling me up the same way. We wanted the same thing.

He put me on my back, and I opened my legs for him to lay between me. He ran his cock along my opening eliciting a moan. He was staring into my eyes, teasing me with his cock, watching every change of expression on my face.

"I can do this forever," I said, quietly.

"We will," Brady said, finally pushing into me.

We made love, and it really was making love, all night long.

EPILOGUE

HAVEN

Reader, he was right. It wasn't easy.

Hollywood wasn't much of a problem - apart from the dangerously intrusive paparazzi and constant fabricated tabloid stories - our age difference was the norm there. Though Brady hated to be part of that cliché. But what could you do? We fell in love. He was called a cheater, a cradle robber. I was called a home wrecker, though his relationship was long dead by the time I came into the picture.

My parents were much more difficult to get on board than I thought. Mom came around within a week after many lengthy conversations and the insistence that I loved him and nothing she said or did would make me end it. My dad wouldn't talk to me for a month. But Brady went out fly fishing with him and suddenly they were the best of friends.

He was also right when he said he couldn't be my passion. I had to find that outside of him. That didn't mean it couldn't begin with him. In

Brady's producing, he'd read a lot of scripts and sometimes, he'd ask for my opinion. I'd read and offer my thoughts. One day I found myself sitting down and rewriting lines of dialogue and then whole scenes. Brady read them and loved them. Days later we were in the midst of writing a screenplay together.

I had always loved reading and writing at school. And, I'd always been a movie addict. I'd never considered trying to write a movie. But once I started, I couldn't stop. I found that passion, that devotion, that purpose that my mom had been pushing me to find. And, it changed my life for the second time.

Nobody's life or love is perfect, but mine was. I counted my blessings to be able to say that I felt happy every single day. I hadn't known it until I knew him, but Brady was everything I'd ever wanted. There were a million reasons why it wouldn't have worked and yet it did. He was my soul mate.

We so easily could've been star crossed. But we found each other and we fought for each other. And it was so worth it.

BRADY

Catalina made finalizing the divorce even more of a nightmare after it all came out. Still, I had a good lawyer, and though Cat threatened to keep my kids from me, she didn't follow through. Haven tried to talk with her, but she wouldn't even see her, and she wouldn't drop the kids off if Haven was there. I knew it hurt Haven.

A few months later, Catalina and the girls were in a car accident. Zola called me for help, but I was out of town. I was terrified. I called the police and the ambulance and then called Haven. She went right over, getting there within minutes. She ended up pulling teeth from Catalina's throat so she could breathe. She got the girls out of the car and kept them safe. It was a horrible thing, and they would never be friends, but Haven had earned her respect.

My kids were the hardest part. They'd continue to be the hardest part for years to come. Mannix was strangely easier to get on board than Zola and Vera. But with time and care, we became a family.

Two years after we met, Haven and I married in front of our closest family and friends on a beach in the Bahamas. That was the longest I could wait. I wanted a ring on both of our fingers. I couldn't hold back my tears as I watched her walk, barefoot in a white silk gown, down the aisle toward me. When we said our vows, Haven was crying, too. I promised to love her forever and she promised the same back, making the promise to my children as well.

HAVEN

Our honeymoon suite was large and luxurious, but the balcony was even better. There was a plush day bed with fluttering white curtains letting in just enough of the warm breeze and the blue moonlight to make it feel like a corner of heaven.

He was touching me differently, still charged but taking his time, like someone put us on slow motion. I wasn't in any hurry.

BRADY

I carried her across the threshold of the room. My wife, finally. I dropped her gently to her feet and closed the door behind us. Before I could turn back to her, she was lifting my shirt off me. She traced her fingers up my back, seemingly following the patterns of ink there. She ran her fingers over my shoulders, and down my chest, pressing her body to me as she traced the curves of my abs down to the trail of hair leading to my belt buckle. I turned around and started to lift her white silk dress up and away.

She had nothing at all on underneath. She was so glorious. I put my hands on her cheeks and brought her big soft lips to mine. I kissed her slowly, taking in her scent, thanking whatever god sent her to me. I ran my hands down her smooth back, over her ass, squeezing it just a little before picking her up again. She wrapped her legs around me, and I carried her, our lips still locked, to the balcony.

I laid her down on the day bed and made quick work of my shoes and slacks. "Come back," she said, reaching out to me. I went back to her. I took her hand and pulled her into my lap, in the middle of the bed. She threw her arms around me and opened my mouth to her. Her thighs squeezed my hips as I brought my hand to her wet pulsing pussy.

She let out a moan and threw her head back a little as she started to ride my fingers. I ran my eyes over her, watching as her breasts heaved, her soft belly quivering a little with her shaky breaths.

Her eyes snapped back to mine, a deeper darker blue than ever. "I want you inside me," she said, and took charge, lining us up and taking me into her cunt.

I let out my own moan at the unbelievable sensation. We kept our eyes locked as I rocked in and out of her.

"You feel so good," I said. "So fucking good." Nothing would ever come close to feeling so good.

HAVEN

My heart was hammering. My whole body was trembling. I couldn't look away from him. He wouldn't let me and I didn't want to. I noticed the sheen on his skin and then mine. Our sweat was gleaming in the moonlight, mingling everywhere we touched.

I looked down, letting my forehead rest against his chest. I watched in the barest of light as the thick length of him pushed in and out of me. We fit so perfectly together.

That divine torturous coiling began in me and I felt him growing and tensing too.

He lifted my chin, bringing my eyes back to him, and my swollen lips back to his before his fingers ran down to slide around my clit. Round and round, they were driving me mad, until I cried out his name and he gave me the pressure I'd been begging for. All my muscles tensed as a deliciously languorous current ran through me.

And, then his face was pressed against my chest. I held onto his head as he drove his cock deep into me, shuddering and groaning as he came inside me. I rubbed at his head and his neck lovingly as he came down.

When he was ready, he brought us back down to the cool sheets to lay facing each other.

"I love you so fucking much," he said, those baby blues intensely staring into mine. "I can't bare it."

"Good," I answered with a tired laugh.

"And you love me, too," he prompted.

"Like crazy," I answered, taking hold of his neck and bringing his lips back to mine.

"Forever?" he asked as we broke apart.

"Forever. I swear," I assured him. "I swear."

* * *

I woke to find him sitting up on the edge of the bed, staring up at the moon. I sat up beside him. "Are you okay?" I asked.

He looked over to me with a smile. He reached down and took my hand, holding it in his. He didn't need to say anything. I had a feeling we were thinking the exact same thing.

BRADY

How the hell did I get so lucky?

About the Author

Christine Darcy is a reader and writer based in Sydney where she lives with her husband and daughter.

Christine J Darcy's TALIA SHAW SERIES is available now:

The Talia Shaw Series follows Talia as she navigates the perils of love and the ups and downs of fame. There will be laughter, love, sex, betrayals, vengeance, forgiveness, weddings, funerals, and finally a happy ending.

In Book One, BRIGHT LIGHTS, Talia Shaw had dreamed one day she'd be flying on a private plane to LA to record an album with her best friends, but when the plane comes crashing down and Talia is the only survivor, she has to do it all on her own.

Talia struggles with her survivor's guilt as she writes her new album and missing her friends as she makes new ones. As her career explodes bringing fame and success, she meets and falls in love for the first time with the cocky, handsome as hell rock star Laurie Siler.

Book Two, LOVE SONGS, picks up where Bright Lights left off, a heartbroken Talia is being reinvigorated on international tour with best friends, Teddy and Lucy. While the rest of the crew is partying, Talia is writing her next album fueled by her breakup with Laurie.

On a break, back in New York, Talia meets gorgeous but serious actor, Jack O'Halloran and a new relationship begins. But it might be a little too much, too soon. No one seems to compare to Laurie. Not Jack, or Jasper, the British actor she meets at the Met Ball and goes home with after a run in with a drunk and rambling Laurie. Nor Romy, the super-rich super model who gets Talia to experiment with her sexuality.

More betrayals, more heart aches and another painful public humiliation on the night of her best friend's wedding will lead Talia to make a big decision about the life she wants to be living and who she wants to live it with...

Talia's story ends in Book Three, HAPPY ENDINGS. Available now on Amazon.com

Sign up to Christine J Darcy's mailing list at www.christinejdarcy.com